"Arise! Sir Humphrey"
ISBN : 0-9547481-1-5

First Published May 2004 by SeaNeverDry Publishing

Copyright © Bobby Hill

The right of Bobby Hill to be identified as the author of this work has been asserted in accordance with sections 77 and 78 of the Copyrights and Patents Act 1988.

Condition of Sale

This book is sold subject to the condition that it will not, by way of trade or otherwise be lent, re-sold, hired out or otherwise circulated without the author's prior consent in any form of binding or cover other than that in which it is published and without a similar condition (including this condition) being imposed on the subsequent purchaser.

Chapter One : The Willing Hands

It began when I was soaking myself in a bubble bath at home, after a particularly gruelling rugby match. I heard the front door shut, and then a rush of movement which heralded Mother's return from some charity activity or other. Then came the urgency as she rushed about her bedroom, the usual cyclone which accompanied her wherever she went.

I thought she would have seen my rugby kit in the hall and saw I was home, but she was moving too fast to notice anything until ... she flung open the bathroom door and saw me, covered in bubbles. She stopped short and quickly wrapped the towel round her - a lost cause. "Tony. I didn't know you were home." She looked about uncertainly.

"Sorry, Mother. Thought you'd have seen my gear in the hall. I was only soaking out some bruises. Give me a couple of seconds and I'll be gone."

"Don't worry. I'm in a hurry darling. Shut your eyes while I get a quick shower."

I did nothing of the kind of course. She dropped the towel, reached inside the cubicle to turn the taps on, while my eyes followed every movement. Her bush was fair, proving that her hair needed no bleaching and growing from it were those long legs and slim ankles that I knew from the many times I had seen her in bathing costumes and bikinis, when on holiday.

What I was now able to appreciate more fully was her very pert bottom, a really tight bum with, above it, the classic sex symbols, a slim, straight back, and protruding from the ribs, a magnificent pair of breasts: They had suckled me, but there was no sign that my teeth or lips had ever grasped those nipples.

They had fed me, but they could still look good on a Page 3 photograph.

I was about to get out of the bath and leave her to it, when she stepped out of the shower, calling to me to shut my eyes again. Her body steaming from the hot water, she bent to pick up her bath towel, wrapped it round herself, giving me another sight of her splendid body, and was gone. I found my hands holding an erection that had sprung up between my legs. I couldn't leave the bathroom now. I would have to give mother a chance to get dressed first.

Our flat had a different configuration from most, probably why mother had chosen it in the first place, or had it chosen for her. I lay back and reflected. Mother had always been mother, old to me, like mothers always are. But she wasn't really. She'd been a child bride, probably a shotgun wedding. I couldn't remember my father, though he was still in touch with Mother, and I suppose supported us. In fact, I didn't really **know** Mother. She was 16 when I was born, so that made her 32. Old to a 12 or a 14 year old, but not so old to a boy of 16. Not when he'd seen her naked.

My earliest recollections had been living with mother at her parents' home in the country. It was from there that I had gone to prep school as a boarder. When Mother collected me at my first half-term, we had a flat in a mansion block that was all on one floor, with one room leading to the next. The hall first, then the sitting room with a dining room and kitchen off it, then mother's bedroom with the big bathroom en suite, then my bedroom at the end. To get to my bedroom I had to go through mother's.

It made sense when I was young. Mother could hear me from her room if I was restive. Then, as I grew older, if she wanted to entertain, she could do so without interruption from me. But as I was still at boarding school, having to go through her room to get to the bathroom seldom caused inconvenience - until now.

I allowed what I thought was enough time for her to dress and got out of the bath. There was still a protuberance in front of me, but the towel hid it as I left the bathroom. I was too early, though. Mother was sitting on her bed, pulling on a stocking as I entered her room. It was a Monet picture come to life. One leg pointed provocatively into the air, her hands drawing a stocking up her thigh, the other, already clad leg, heel resting on the floor, dragging the eye to the white flesh between it and the black lace of her panties, small enough to allow some of her blonde pubes to creep out. I caught a glimpse of her breasts protruding over a black lacy bra. The picture, black panties, black suspender belt, a half rolled on black stocking was one which a porno magazine would have paid big money for. She looked even sexier than when she was naked.

I could feel the movement under the towel but neither of us said anything. She paused in her dressing as I muttered something and went through into my own bedroom. I began rubbing myself dry, curling the towel round my back, that protuberance still sticking out when I remembered the mirror.

There had always been a dressing table against one wall of mother's bedroom with its mirrors angled. The communicating door had always been left open, as it was now, so that from her bed she could see into my room and my bed.

She was there in all my youthful arrogance. She was bent over, straightening her seams when she caught sight of me in the mirror. She hadn't put her dress on, and I could see the length of her legs, the whiteness of her skin between the tops of her stockings and her pants, the top of her breasts as they thrust out from her bra and imagined the shape of her bottom as it thrust out behind.

One of us had to do something. I moved backwards out of the line of sight, then hurriedly threw some clothes on. When I'd dressed I went through to Mother's tidy as usual bedroom into the sitting room, she stood sipping a sherry. She didn't offer me one though I guessed she knew I helped myself to the occasional drink.

"What are your plans for this evening?" she asked in the conversational tone of a realistic woman who really wanted to know, as I moved around the room.

"Not sure, yet" and indeed, I didn't know. "The Grosvenor boys are trying to persuade their parents to go out so they can hold a party."

Gordon and Gerald Grosvenor lived in a mansion, ideal for the informal parties we liked to go to. For 'party' read 'orgy'. School had taught us a great deal.

"Will there be any girls there?"

"Oh, Yes. Some of the girls from school were at the match. They'll come and bring their friends. It'll be great fun, if it happens."

I sincerely hoped it did. I would be able to get rid of the weight, not exactly on my mind, but the thought was ever-present.

There was a ring at the doorbell, the taxi Mother was expecting. She finished her drink and stood up.

"I hope you have a nice time," she said as she moved towards the door to the hall. Then she paused and turned round. "We'll move that dressing table tomorrow. I don't need to keep an eye on you at night now, you're a **big** boy.

As she said the word 'big' there was a half-smile on her face, and her eyes flicked towards my crutch. "I'll move it tonight" I answered, and added rather daringly, "I wish I had discovered its advantages before."

She wasn't sure what I meant, and let the remark pass, but I continued, "I've seen lots of naked ladies on the beaches, and we often see girls naked at school, they probably see us without any clothes on as well, running about the gym and the changing rooms. Of course we look at them, but I've never seen anyone as beautiful as my mother."

I was certain she blushed. "On that note, I'll say 'Goodnight'. "I don't think I've ever had a better compliment."

The door closed, she was gone.

What I had told her was true. What I didn't add was that I'd also seen many of the mistresses naked. My school was a progressive one, a co-educational boarding school that gave a great degree of licence to the pupils, and the staff.

Whilst the age of consent was still 16 for a girl, and presumably for a boy also, the school's view was a more liberal one. The 16 year rule only applied to boys outside the school. Boys in the school were exempt. The area between under-age girls and boys was deliberately vague.

The school view was that maturity brought responsibility. When the girl students reached puberty matron offered them a course on the pill, so that should they want to put the theory taught in the sex education lessons into practice, there would be no repercussions.

Many of them did. Sex was not encouraged, neither was it discouraged. The school stood in its own grounds of many acres, and was surrounded by woods, rivers even lakes, all within easy cycling distance. Each Saturday there was a disco attended by those from the fourth form and above, the over 16s.

Sunday mornings were when most pupils did their cycling. 'Going for some exercise', it was called as they cycled off with their dancing partner of the night before.

I hoped one of those girls would be at the party that evening, if it happened. It would be a relief in more ways than one. As it happened, I was disappointed. The Grosvenor parents returned early to cast a blight on the party and though Helen, one of the favourites from school, was as enthusiastic as me, there was no place for us to go. It was just a quick grope in the back of a taxi as I took her home.

My frustrations of the day vanished when I got home, but were soon replaced by apprehension. As soon as I put my key in the lock I knew something was wrong. The flat was in darkness. We always left the lights on.

Of course my first thought was burglars. I was big for a 16 year old but didn't fancy the idea of meeting a man with a knife or gun. I felt for a walking stick that I knew was left in a corner, and found it. I felt happier with a weapon, held it in front of me and rushed into the sitting room. My fingers found the light switch. To my surprise, the lights came on; I'd expected them to be deliberately fused.

My fears were realised when I saw Mother sprawled face down on a couch in the sitting room, her dress awry, parts of it above her waist revealing her stocking tops. I didn't even give a thought to the sexiness of her posture. I feared the worst as I ran across to her. Without thinking I plunged my hand down her dress to feel her heart. It was beating strongly, but the breast under my hand sent shivers down my spine. She was alive, no obvious signs of having been attacked. Was it a matter for the police?

Television and video were still there, no obvious signs of pieces missing. I opened Mother's handbag. Her wallet with a large sum of money was there, her necklace was still round her neck, rings still on her fingers. No. Nothing seemed to have been taken.

I checked her heart. Again, still beating strongly, I allowed myself a squeeze of her nipple. So what was wrong? There was only drink left. Mother was drunk. She'd got home, turned the lights out and collapsed on the couch, a situation I just couldn't believe, Mother would never allow herself to be intoxicated. But there it was. Now came the problem I had been dodging. What do I do? Leave her there? Would I have left my girlfriend there, a friend there, my father there, anybody I knew there? Of course not. I'd undress them and put them to bed. So should I leave my Mother there?

I picked her up and carried her into her bedroom. The zip was on the back of her dress, and as I pulled it down I noticed the label, Schiaparelli. Even I knew that name. I took her shoes off, and undid the zip. The dress came down over her shoulders down to her waist. I rolled her onto her back, exposing once again her bra and the globes of her breasts, rising gently as she breathed. Getting the dress past her hips was not so easy, I had to inch it down, past one hip and then the other until it was at her thighs. The next part would be easy, but though I had a feeling of guilt, I still had to pause and savour what I was seeing. There were her breasts, hidden by her bra. I couldn't remember whether her tan went as far as her nipples, and though I could look with impunity. I decided to wait, giving my attention instead to the black strap of her suspender belt round her waist, and below it, as I eased the dress down, the pair of very fine lace edged panties, hardly big enough to hide her pussy.

I smoothed the dress down her legs until it was off. In the wardrobe was its coat-hanger and cover. I hung it on the hangar and held it up, The creases would drop out now.

Then came the stockings. I had fantasized about this very act. Now I was going to do it in reality.

I undid each suspender and rolled them down, taking care not to ladder them. I placed these in the laundry basket. I was able to undo the suspender belt by sliding my hands under and around her waist. I slid the belt off, caressing it with my lips as it entered the laundry basket and joined the stockings. Just bra and panties left. I wished I had a camera. The bra next. Once again I slipped my arms around her to find the clip, squeezing her breasts with my arms as I did so, but there was no clip. Several seconds of confusion then, of course, it was at the front. I'd heard about front loaders. But this was the first time I'd experienced them. Gave me some sort of clue to Mother's lifestyle. Made it much easier to get to them, They should be compulsory for all girls.

I threw the bra into the laundry basket and gazed admiringly at her breasts. True, they had suckled me, but there was no sign on her body even of child bearing never mind child rearing. Even though she was lying on her back, the orbs of her breasts were still proud, the nipples challenging all comers.

There remained only her panties. They came last. There was hardly anything of them, just a whisper of silk and lace. I eased it down over her buttocks and down her legs, off one foot and then the other. I put them to my mouth, and savoured the smell and taste of her. I put everything but the panties into the laundry basket, the panties went under the pillow in my bedroom.

I lifted Mother up and moved the duvet from under her. I was about to cover her it when I lost the bet I had made with myself. I kissed her breasts once again and felt them harden. Then I slipped my hand down to her pussy. It was wet. My fingers stroked her vagina and automatically her legs parted. Even in sleep her sensuality couldn't be suppressed. I moved my fingers in and out, and her vulva moved with them. Her clitoris found my fingers and introduced itself.

It was as big as a cottonwool bud, and my fingers squeezed it. She moaned, which caused me an anxious moment, but she was still fast asleep. The moan was one of pleasure, but I could give her greater pleasure. I knelt at her feet, lifted her buttocks and placed my head between her legs. I could feel the heat of her passion as my tongue found her pussy. Past the inner lips to where her vulva, even in sleep, gripped my tongue. Her clitoris was erect and first my lips then my teeth teased it. She gave a sigh. Her buttocks jerked in my hands and I felt her come. My face was wet from her juices and I drank what I could of them. She calmed and I knew it was time to go. T put her legs together, moved her into the centre of the bed and covered her with the duvet.

In my own room I lay on my bed, wondering what would have happened if I'd taken the final step. My erection had been banging my legs for hours, and there had been, still was, a chance to quieten it that I hadn't taken. There was only one alternative.

Not surprisingly, I was up first next morning. I went through Mother's room and paused at her bed. She had turned over during the night. Her eyes flickered, registered on me, and then closed again. I made some tea, put some toast in the toaster and bacon under the grill. I took a cup of tea into Mother and left it on the bedside table.

The smell of the cooking bacon was fragrant. I had buttered the toast, laid the breakfast table and was frying eggs when Mother entered the kitchen. She had showered, and put on a slight touch of make-up, but her eyes were red.

"That smells good. You can be mother today, I'll just relax and have a restful time. I feel like death."

I said nothing, but she wanted to clear the air. "Last night was one best forgotten. I was at San Lorenzo's for dinner, and I think one of the 'gentlemen' an emphasis on the word 'gentleman', laced my drink. He probably thought he'd take me home and to bed, but he was unlucky, I made it home."

I poured a cup of the coffee I had been percolating, and presented her with a plate of bacon, eggs, tomatoes and mushrooms. "That's gorgeous" she said, and began tucking in. She was hungry, she'd had no dinner.

Between mouthfuls she continued her story. "I hadn't even started the first course when I began to feel ill. The fool couldn't even do that right, probably been pumping one of his sons about drugs, they're always in and out of the courts. Gave me an overdose." without pausing, she shot the question at me, "Take it you put me to bed?"

I nodded. "When I got home, the lights were off and you were lying on the couch, absolutely unconscious. My first thought was burglars, then call the police in case you were in some sort of Ecstasy fit, but you seemed to be sleeping so soundly that I didn't."

"Just as well" said Mother. Had the police come round and started asking question on who I'd been with at dinner, and where, a certain City broker and his friends would have a lot of questions to answer today. In any case, I bet he had a restless night, and he'll have a few more in the future. His tactics are not the approved ones."

It was the very first adult conversation we'd had. Yesterday's events had altered our relationship. I was no longer a boy, not quite a man but a young man, one who had traveled widely, seen much and grown up. She was no longer an 'Augusta' mother… an old woman, but a young lady, she'd grown younger, I'd grown older, and we were now on a brother and sister level rather than mother and son.

"Did you have trouble undressing me?" It was a bald question demanding a straight bald answer." "Not really. You hadn't got much in the way of clothes on. The only problem was whether I should leave you or not. I could have laid you on the bed covered you up. It would have ruined your dress, but so what? Then I thought that if it was anybody else, father, girlfriend, mate or whatever, I'd put him or her to bed properly. You've done it for me, so why not you? "Anyway," I said boldly. I wanted to. I enjoyed it. Remember I said I hadn't seen a woman as beautiful as you. I was able to look at you, closely."

There was a long pause. She picked at her bacon and eggs, then picked up her coffee cup, held it in both hands in front of her face and asked the question to which she already knew the answer. My earlier answers had told her what she needed to know if she wanted to keep a distance. Asking it brought us closer together.

"Was it a dream or did you.. "

I didn't let her finish. "Yes. I teased you. But I didn't do anything else."

She knew what I meant.

"Why didn't you?"

"I did want to. I had an enormous hard-on, but it wouldn't have been fair. You can only do that to a girl if she wants it. I would have been as bad as the man who gave you the drug!"

She took another sip of her coffee before asking, "Where did you learn to do all that? You're not supposed to know about things like that until you're married" adding bitterly "not even then sometimes."

I couldn't help giggling. "Mother, there's a book called the Khama Sutra on the bookshelf. At the back of the video cabinet are some films, hidden away for some reason, that are quite explicit. I go to a co-ed school which has a sex education lesson each week in which we are the models. Not to mention a procession of gorgeous Scandinavian ladies you employed as au pairs when I was here on holiday. Now, how do you think I learned these things"?

She laughed outright. "Touche. I'd forgotten all about the au pairs. I hope some young ladies are getting the benefit of this education!!"

I think so."

"Good. In that case, perhaps I could have a pair of panties returned. They're Janet Reger, and though there isn't much of them, they're quite expensive." "I know. I bought them for your birthday."

"Oops. Sorry. Of course you did. I often wondered how you had the nerve to go into the shop and buy them?"

"I took one of the girls from school with me. She thought they were for her."

"But what happened when she found they weren't?" "She wasn't disappointed. When we got outside, I made an excuse, went back into the shop and ordered another set, with a smaller bra, for her."

Mother looked down at where her bosom was hidden by her dressing gown.

"You mean, you not only knew her bra size but mine as well?"

"If I was going to buy you underwear, there was no point in buying the wrong size was there? All I had to do was look into the laundry basket for one of your bras."

"Yes, but what about the girl? Who is she? How old is she? How do you know the size of her breasts? Was it her birthday too?"

"Oh, Mother. She's Helen Fortesque. She's one of our group. You've met her."

"You mean Judge Fortesque's daughter?"

"That's her. She's my partner in sex education lessons. It wasn't her birthday but there was a special reason."

That answer opened up a minefield of questions which Mother decided to ignore.

" I'm not going to ask any more questions, in case I'm frightened by the fact that my young son is no longer a boy. He's a grown-up and it's going to take some getting used to. I'm going to spend the day at home. You go out and terrorise someone else Anyway, where are my panties?"

"Under my pillow."

That really gave her something to think about, but she decided to say nothing.

I poured her some more coffee, went to the hall for the Sunday papers and brought them back. There was no point in having a shower. It was rugby training that afternoon, so I had a quick wash before donning my tracksuit. I had several sets of rugby strip, and it was only a matter of collecting the boots from the hall. I bent over Mother for a quick kiss on the cheek, got a glimpse of her breasts underneath her dressing gown, only just stopped myself from giving them a squeeze

It was if she read my thought. She turned her chair round so she was facing me, undid the bow of my tracksuit trousers and pulled them down. I took a deep breath as her hands slipped inside my boxer shorts and pulled them down also. She looked at my equipment and I looked down her cleavage to where I could see her breasts rising and falling in her excitement. She put her hands out and held my cock. Like an inner tube being inflated it began to rise and rise until it filled both her hands. She stroked the foreskin back and forth then pulled it right back. Its shiny head glistened.

"So this is what I almost felt last night?" she said. stroking it gently. "I think I might have woken up if this had gone into me." I could feel it pulsing as she stroked it, so could she. She pulled, forcing me to drop to my knees, and took one hand away so that the folds of her dressing gown were out of the way. I had a view of her pussy, the drops of her juice on her hairs glistening. The lips were moist. I moved to kiss it, but she pushed me back.

"Not now. I just want to feel what it is I brought into the world.."

She moved forward on the chair so that I could enter her. She rode it for a couple of strokes, then pushed me away. Abruptly, she stood up and closed her gown around her.

"You'll need your strength for rugby" she said. "Where's your training ground?"

"Battersea Park. Why?"

"Thought I might wander over if I get bored."

"Do come. A lot of the girls turn up, they get turned on watching all these muscular legs charging about, particularly when I get into the scrum, One girl told me she fantasised being in the middle of the scrum, with all the bottoms and thighs around her. She's brazen enough to do it too".

The rugby team were the elite of the school. The players could take their pick of the girls. The cachet of having a rugby player on your arm at the discos was enormous. At school functions Helen wore me. In private too, when nothing more interesting offered. She could match me at everything.

It was great.

A few old pupils turned up to watch the training. Battersea Park was convenient. They'd go to the away matches in the London area, but one couldn't blame them for missing home matches at school, it wasn't that easy to get to. Helen's family lived in London. She had no trouble getting to Battersea, particularly as she used her father's car and chauffeur. She was at the ground when I arrived. I used buses, bikes were so easily stolen. She broke away from her friends to give me a greeting. It was a deep French kiss that left my knees trembling, particularly as her hand had found my crutch and was stroking my prick into life.

Having got it hard she broke off. "We'd better get it made tonight" she said. "I'm that randy I could screw you on the pitch."

"But what would Daddy say?"

"He'd probably give me three months, to get tired of you."

I took her arm to walk her back to her chums, slipping my hand underneath her bum so that I gave her a quick lift in the air, my fingers hard against her quim.

"Bastard!" she said with a smile, letting her hand drop back until it found my goolies and giving them a hard squeeze which left me doubled over. Life with Helen at 16 was exciting. Someone was going to marry her and would either become Prime Minister or a drunk.

"You've not met my cousins, Daphne and Dolores, they're twins."

There wasn't much doubt about that. If they weren't already causing mayhem among their boyfriends, swapping when they fancied it, they would do at our school.

"Daddy's already got an Agnes, a Beatrice and a Catherine" said Daphne, or it could have been Dolores, by way of explanation, Mummy's pregnant again and sixteen years later we're all hoping it will be an Edward. We think it's his last chance."

"Mummy says it is" said Daphne/Dolores. "Says she's not going through another pregnancy. She's certain Daddy deliberately punctured the F.L. so as to have another try."

"It's the title." said Dolores/Daphne. "Perhaps the off-beat example will work. I hope so."

Like her sister, she was a testament to the success of the dental profession's ability to sell barbed wire to parents. Her mouth looked like the pictures we all saw of the trenches on the Somme, barbed wire and concrete block teeth.

Nature always compensates and he pays double in boobs. Even under the Barbour coats their chest development was obvious. I would have to introduce them to Harvey of the Fifth, the school photographer. He was already making a name for himself in Fleet Street, He took all the official school pictures, but he had a sideline going in unofficial snaps. Any girl with a reasonable amount of looks, and breasts to match, was invited to pose for him, topless. "Let me photograph you while they're at their peak" he would say. "Have a photograph to show your grandchildren how you looked when you were their age." Most of the girls with looks at school had been photographed, some had appeared in the Sun and the Mirror, but as neither they or their family read either paper, no-one was any the wiser.

Harvey would love it. Great Page 3. 'The Honourable Miss Dolores Ramsbottom rests her breasts on the five barred gate at the home of her father, the 10th Earl, while she enjoys life in the country'.

My mind had slipped out of gear, but I did a quick rewind with the inbuilt tape-recorder and played it back to where Daphne/Dolores was saying, "He's the Tenth Earl and he's rather bitter that he hasn't been able to sire the eleventh."

"Who knows how many of the previous lot haven't been the result of a passing minstrel or shepherd or whatever, while the old man was away on the Crusades?" put in Helen. Her father was only a life Peer. "Often wonder myself" said Daphne/Dolores. "Mother hasn't got any tits, don't know how she fed the two of us, and if you look in the picture gallery at home you won't find any Countess with cleavage. So where did these come from?" as she gazed down at the ample frontal development of her and her sister.

"Bet you don't find anyone complaining" I put in. "No, agreed Daphne/Dolores. Once I take the ironwork off my teeth its all systems go. Some boys though, like to feel the metal rubbing against their..."

"They're joining our school next term" cut in Helen, putting an end to any ideas I might have entertained about the twins. She had funny ideas about playing with her friends. Helen was 18, and would be going on to university. The twins were my age, 16. 1 enjoyed school. We had never been forced to do anything. We had our own rules at school. If you wanted to, you could do anything, as long as you didn't offend anyone or, as a royal said, 'frighten the horses'.

"Helen's told us so much about your school that we badgered Daddy into letting us change. Can't wait to join in one of your end of term celebrations. Wild."

Helen or no, I made a mental promise to myself that by the next end-of-term party I would have myself a session with the Double Dees, as I christened them, and their double Ds. My lechery showed. Helen always picked up my vibes.

"Watch out you two. He fancies you. If he's got enough lead left in his pencil, after I've finished with him at the next end of term do, he's yours."

The duo giggled as if fearful, but unwittingly, Helen had issued a challenge which they, and I, would take up.

I left them for the changing rooms. A piece of pasteboard fluttered to the changing room floor as I took my gear out of the bag. It bore Daphne's name and phone number. That was neat. I didn't see her put it there. I memorised the number... Helen took no prisoners.

The Ramsbottom sisters got their introduction into the school world immediately after our training session. We'd played 30 minutes rugby, had done circuit training for another 30 and were covered in mud and sweat when we piled into the changing rooms. They weren't the only girls there. Several had lined the touchlines and had retreated to the changing rooms as it grew dark. They just kept out of the way as the players stripped, threw their sweaty gear at their girlfriends and jumped into the hot, communal bath.

There were shouts of, "Dawn, wash my back, Come on Hazel, get the soap." The routine was the same on match days, the girls rolled their sleeves up and scrubbed us down after the game, much to the chagrin of the visiting team who didn't have similar supporters.

There were times when the girls jumped into the bath as well, but this wasn't one of them.

The Double Dees took no time to adjust to the sight of some 20 men, parading their private bits uncaringly in front of them. They fell to scrubbing backs, and fronts, with gusto, and even though Helen was giving me her own best attention, I felt a third hand caress my privates. The half smile on Daphne's lips showed me whose hand it had been.

She and Dolores were just as enthusiastic when it came to drying us. They were going to be real acquisitions to the rugby team. Daphne would have given me attention, but Helen beat her to it. Instead she concentrated on the scrum half whose back, chest, calves, ankles and feet were bone dry. There must have been some problem with the rest of his anatomy because she was spending so much time on it.

Because there were fewer supporters than players, school rules insisted that no player be unattended, so most girls found themselves drying two boys. It never caused any problems, there was never any question of jealousy. Like the after-term party, what happened there was one thing, the outside world was another. The Ramsbottom sisters were in their element and, having ensured their arrival at school would be an easy one, Helen was ready to concentrate her attention to the next thing on her mind. My cock. She had a minute inspection, which involved running her tongue around its rim, during the drying process. I noticed that her pupils Daphne and Dolores had found the same treatment necessary for their patients.

"Let's go!" said Helen.

"Where?" I asked. I've always been curious.

"Your place" she answered.

That did take me by surprise. "Whaa.."

"It's O.K. It's your mother's idea. She rang me, asked if we'd any plans for later. I said 'No' so she said to come round and bring a few of the gang with us."

"Where did she get your number?"

"Easy. Dad's in the phone book."

That was a relief. It meant my diary, and list of phone numbers were still safe.

"How many are invited?"

"As many as want to come, she said. No limit. She's getting Justin de Blank to send the food round, and she said that she's not going to check what's in any glasses."

"Have you told anybody?"

"Not yet. Waited until I'd told you. Do you want to do it?"

"Of course. Tell them."

Demure though she looked, Helen could, had she wanted, become a parade ground colonel.

"Listen! I shall say this only once. Party tonight. All invited. Everything provided. Don't bring anything, just yourselves."

Typical of Helen, she had already written out my address on slips of paper which she passed out. There was sure to be a big attendance at this party. The private one would be in my bedroom. For once, it would be an advantage, mother's bed would be the cloakroom. "Can we give you a lift?" asked one of the Double Dees.

"Don't tell me you've got a cab waiting?" I asked. "No. We've got the car. Daddy wasn't going to let us out without a chaperone, so we've got George looking after us."

"Perfect" said Helen. "Let's go."

Two more girls joined us in the run to the limo, but there was space enough and to spare for another couple, and I wished they were blokes. Somehow, Daphne of the Double Dees, had manoeuvered Helen, as the eldest, into the front passenger seat. The partition had gone up to isolate her from what would happen in the back. I could have struggled, but there are times when males have to lie back and think of England.

My trousers were off and while two pairs of hands were coaxing my organ into life, a smooth pair of buttocks were lowered gently onto my face. My arms had been held, but I shrugged them off so that I could position that juicy pussy properly. The tongues which had been urging life into my penis were being replaced by the real thing. I was sure it was Daphne who was the first to lower herself on to my cock, just as I was certain it was Dolores' clitoris that I was nibbling. They changed round, and I was able to explore the thighs and breasts which were being rubbed on me. I heard one girl suppress a gasp as she orgasmed. Daphne told me later that it was Dolores who had beaten her to it. As it happened, there was a traffic jam on Battersea Bridge, so there was plenty of time for me to savour their delights too. We established a routine, one would sit on my cock while I jiggled their breasts, until I brought her off, when another would take their place. While I fucked her as hard as I could from that position, Daphne refused to orgasm.

"I'm saving it for later."

The following day, when I took my rugby kit out to wash, I found four pairs of panties wrapped up in my shorts. But that was later, this was tonight. I was enjoying every man's fantasy, four gorgeous, more than willing girls, prepared to do anything that they haven't done already. The car started to move, the jam was clearing. The girls enjoyed pulling my knickers and trousers over my legs. Daphne made herself responsible for tucking my penis in, and zipping up the fly. "See you later" she whispered to it.

I didn't doubt that she would, despite Helen's interest. Once over the bridge, it was minutes only to the flat . I led the way, past the commissionaire who was looking speculatively at the group and their dress, if a mini-skirt of Anita's, topped by a tee shirt, an anorak flung over one arm can be called dressing. It was all they had on as I knew from experience. But they had long legs, breasts that bounced and they were bubbling with excitement at what they had just done, and what they were going to do.

"Three at a time in the lift" said Helen, resuming responsibility for her charges. "Two come with me." She pressed the button to call it down. It was, I explained, very temperamental, and had been known to jam between floors. Even as I was saying the words, I tried to swallow them. I saw the look Daphne flashed across to Dolores.

"Helen took her charges into the lift, leaving, not unexpectedly, the Double Dees in my care. Daphne was already undoing the buttons on her blouse revealing her deep cleavage. "How do you jam the lift between floors" she asked conversationally. "Do you think it might happen when we're in it?"

"Please" I begged. "It's Mother's party. No-one will believe it happened accidentally, particularly when they see who was in the lift with me. They'll probably call the police and have me done for rape. Anyway, haven't you had enough of me for tonight?" "No way" she said, and dropped her hand down to grasp my crutch. "I want lots more of this fellow." She was still grasping it as the lift arrived. "I'll behave if you promise to come to lunch tomorrow. A deal?"

"A deal" I replied.

As I pressed the button to start the lift, I slipped a hand into her blouse. A breast leapt into my hand. Daphne bent over to bite my ear. "Rapist" she murmured. "Are you going to fuck me properly tonight, or has Helen got first call."

" 'Fraid so" I answered.

"Leave some for tomorrow then." She gave me a final squeeze as the lift door opened, and did up some buttons, as I led them into our flat.

I found myself in the role of host, being introduced to Mother's friends and then finding myself looking after them. Fortunately, Helen joined me and we became a double act, introducing the younger set to the older. Mother had briefed them on what was being worn now. It was Anita's and tee shirts, the occasional blouse, a denim skirt or tight trousers. No V.P.L's or bras.

Mother was the star. She had made an effort to play herself down, choosing a long dress which hid her legs and went up to her throat. No cleavage, but she still shone. The others were like satellites around the sun though there were some good looking girls among them. I wondered if she had invited the man who had tried it on with her last night, and later found out she had.

Once I'd done the host bit. It was time to take care of Helen. As two more guests arrived, we took their coats, deposited them on Mother's bed and carried on into my bedroom. For the first time, I closed the door.

I didn't turn the light on, there was enough coming in from outside after I drew the curtains.

When I turned round, Helen was already lying on my bed, naked. She was slimmer than Mother. Her breasts were still growing as were her calves and her thighs.

I didn't wait to take any of my clothes off. I gave her a perfunctory kiss on the lips, kissed each breast, squeezing the other as I did so, then lifted her buttocks and her pussy to my face. Her squeal as I nibbled her clitoris would have been heard in Mother's bedroom had anyone been there. (I didn't know then, but the Double Dees were there, listening to everything). I paused for a second to strip off my shirt and trousers, then gave my full attention to Helen's pussy. I was pulling at her clit with my lips when I remembered what was underneath my pillow. Mother's panties. I paused in my endeavours, not a wise thing to do as Helen was susceptible to every nuance in love-making. By then the urgency had left her, though it was still with me.

"What's wrong darling?" she murmured, as I lifted my head up.

"Nothing sweet. Fancy a glass of champagne?"

I had seen the ice-bucket and the bottle in the corner. The champagne flutes were on the bedside cabinet. After opening the bottle, I slipped a hand under the pillow to find.. nothing. Slight panic, and while Helen was taking my pants and socks off I tried the other pillow, also empty. At some risk, I lifted both up to make a backrest for Helen. The sheet was clean of any black, filmy object.

Unaware of how much action it had been through, how many Gardens of Eden it had already visited that night, Helen poured champagne over my cock and began to wash it. The coldness made it shrink, but her lips were there to bring it back to full fruition.

She loved to toy with it, pull it, stroke it, suck it, nibble it. Her favorite lollypop she called it. She often went to sleep with it in her mouth. It was as big as it ever would be now. It had wanted pussy last night, given a surfeit of it this evening, and now it wanted to speak for itself. She knew it.

"Let's fuck" she said, and pulled one of the pillows down under her bottom, lifting it up and letting me have greater penetration. I moved on top of her and her hand grasped my cock, giving it a few familiar strokes before guiding it into her pussy. I put one arm behind her neck and bent to give her a long, lascivious kiss, while my left hand gripped her right breast. At the right moment, as my strokes became deeper, my fingers gripped her nipple and twisted it. Her legs tightened around my waist, I twisted her nipple even harder, and then came her orgasm. I learned later that the Double Dees thought I had beaten her, so loud was her cry. I didn't hear it, I was coming at that time. I could only hear Helen calling "Yes. Yes. Fill me. Fill me." I gave her everything I had until, spent, it slipped out of her pussy to lie harmless on her thigh.

That was the moment Helen enjoyed. I was helpless, not even wanting to move. She pushed me, so that I rolled onto my back. Then she slid down the bed until she was opposite the tiny, damp little whelk. She found the little thing and began to tease it. She treated it as a challenge, how long would it take before she got it big enough for her teeth to take over?

Once her lips began their massage it was no time at all before it was ready for service. By then, her pussy was being kissed and her clitoris activated.

This time however, was not the right time for one of our all-night sessions. Our thirsts had been slaked. It was time to join the party.

We used champagne to wash our naughty bits, dried ourselves on paper hankies, dressed, and were on our way to the door when I remembered. "Give me your panties. I want them under my pillow." "Good idea. We'll swap." We swapped underwear, but once again the temptation was too much. Before I could put my trousers on, Helen sank to her knees and took my penis in her mouth. She fell back, drawing me with her. I turned as her legs opened and she pleaded "Suck me. Kiss me."

I buried my face in her pussy. My tongue had barely entered her and kissed her clitoris before she burst out into a screaming orgasm, which brought the Double Dees storming in to her assistance.

"Jeeesus!" said Daphne. "All that from a bonk!! Wow. Tony, you sure are something."

They came into the room and shut the door behind them. There was still some champagne left. We shared it. There wasn't much point in covering ourselves up, in any event the twins had already made a physical inspection of my privates as well as a study of them in the changing room. It didn't stop Daphne slipping her hand under my still damp bits and weighing them in her hand.

"Hands off" said Helen. "Not in public. We're an item in public."

"This isn't public" Daphne rejoined, pulling my foreskin back and bending over to give it a little kiss. "It is a party and you've had your share, besides it's the only one here." "Move over" said Dolores.

Daphne gave it a little kiss before surrendering her place to Dolores, whose hands were soon cupping my cock.

"Don't I get some say in all this?" I complained. "Just be grateful" said Daphne pushing me back so that I was stretched out on my bed. In seconds she was sitting on my face, she hadn't even got to take her panties off, they were in my sports bag. My tongue once again was nibbling her clitoris while her sister was doing her best to wank me into life. I could hear Helen laughing. I'd have thought she would be jealous, but no.

Daphne took pity on me and got off me. She made no attempt to cover herself, lounging on my bed, stockings and suspenders temptingly on display as well as a moist labia. She ran a finger down it, and when I did nothing, sighed dramatically, and slid off the bed, leaving a moist patch behind.

"What's it like out there?" I asked.

"Pretty good" said Dolores. "The lights are really turned down. Hard to know who's doing what to who."

"Which reminds me" said I, once again putting my trousers on, wondering when they would make them with Velcro fastenings for situation like this. "One of the blokes out there was rather crude to Mother. Slipped her a Mickey Finn to try and get a legover. I'll point him out and perhaps you two could play a game with him?"

"No trouble" said Daphne. "It's the sort of thing we specialise in."

Chapter Two : Eager Au Pairs

Mother had pointed out the man she thought was Mickey Finn. About 30, good looking, Armani suit, good shoes, but he was a grabber. He was the one who would join couples as the guy went off to get the drinks, chat the girl up and try to get her away. It actually worked sometimes. The Double Dees didn't need any pointing out. He must have thought it was Christmas when they 'found' him. They were all over him. A couple, still only involved in the groping stage found themselves on their feet, whilst the Double Dees and their new disciple took over the couch they had been occupying.

It isn't usual to see men at parties wearing braces. Even among the older guys there was always the chance of a pull. The Grope had kept his jacket on, to keep them concealed - until then. But as Dolores joined him they were somehow separated from his trousers. It turned out that they had disappeared altogether, which accounted for his strange departure later that evening.

Dolores had taken-the opportunity of inspecting the bathroom cabinet and found a bottle of baby oil. The subdued lights were ideal. He made no complaint as Dolores pulled his trousers and underpants down, applied oil liberally to her hand and began entertaining his member whilst sitting on his legs, so that not only did her dress provide some cover – not that anyone was caring – but that his knees should feel the warmth and moistness of her pussy. Her panties were in my sports bag.

Daphne had been more direct. Her pussy was positioned directly over his mouth, which left it no alternative but to engage in a bout of cunnilingus. He was doing a good job, as she told us later. But, having reached a minor climax herself, she took time out to let him enjoy himself and the taste of her pussy. Then, at a signal to Dolores she let out a fart she had been saving. It was heard even outside the confines of her dress. "Pardon" she said politely, before letting another one go.

The first had been the signal for Dolores, whose efforts on Mickey Finn's penis had intensified. However, even a well-oiled 'Brillo' pad which she then introduced into the proceedings, couldn't disguise its abrasiveness when used with exertion on an upstanding penis.

It took Mickey Finn several long seconds before he was able to escape from the confines, and aroma, of Daphne's dress, throw Dolores off and stagger - where? His trousers were round his ankles, he had almost suffocated under Daphne's weight and farts, and his cock felt like a carrot that had come against a vegetable scraper. Holding up his trousers, he fled. Cab drivers in the West End are very understanding.

The events had not gone unobserved by Mother. The lights were so low that it was difficult to see anyone, but I spotted her up against the bar, her hand against her mouth as she stifled her laughter. The Double Dees were posing, Dolores demonstrating the weapon which had taken such an edge off Mickey's sexual appetite. There were flecks of blood on it, not surprisingly.

"Thank you" said Mother as I joined her. "I think he'll realise where the lesson came from, and I don't think he'll try it on any other girl."

A fair amount of mingling was going on between the two groups, Mother's and mine. Anita and Diana the other two girls who had ravished me in the car, had found a couple from the stockbroker brigade, Porsche and BMWs for sure, and were allowing themselves to be gently groped. Their transport home was guaranteed.

Some of the females among Mother's friends with toy boys in mind, had fastened onto the rugby players, and had their hands inside their shirts, stroking their chests. If they thought they were doing the seducing, they were in for a surprise.

Daphne and Dolores were the first to go, giving me a meaningful look as they left, to prepare their lunch for the following day. They gave Helen a lift, chauffeur George had waited for them. Their example was soon followed by those who thought they were in with a chance, and then those who made last minute arrangements with the other wallflowers.

Whoever was left cuddling and sleeping in the corners could stay there till morning. Mother was too late to take possession of her own bed, a couple were fast asleep on the remaining coats.

Mine was the only room left. I'd made sure of that by closing and locking the door behind us as Helen and I left it. I took her by the hand and led her into it locking the door once more. She sank down on the bed. "Good party?"

"Wonderful. To think some of your friends, men and women, are going to be regular visitors to our school." I bent over to kiss her. It was meant to be a kiss on the cheek, but she moved her face and we were deep in one of those kisses that has only one outcome. Even when our lips parted it was to kiss eyes, ears, cheeks and then as I moved my hands to pull up the blouse she was wearing, her breasts.

I nuzzled them, running my tongue in the valley between them kissing first one then the other, biting, sucking as she pushed them up to me. "Bite them, bite the nipples" she was saying. She was struggling to pull her blouse over her head, without interrupting my a assault on her bosom. At last she succeeded and then pulled my shirt off. We took minutes off for me to undo my Anitas and pull them down, sticking a toe in one sock at a time to pull them off, and then do the same to her skirt. She lay back on the bed voluptuously, her arms straight out, her breasts thrusting upwards, her pussy hidden by a pair of panties. I leaned over her, inserted a finger on each side and eased them down. She lifted her bum as they came past it. I slowly drew them the length of her legs until they were free. I raised them to my lips and kissed them.

"You won`t need those" she said. "You can't take them every time you peel them off me."

I dropped them and then went to bury my face in her crutch. Her legs opened to receive me.

"Turn round darling" she said. "Straddle me."

I did, and Humphrey was in her hands. She rolled me so that we were lying side by side. I watched her as she explored Humphrey and his two friends with her tongue, stroking the foreskin up and down. She toyed with them while I was exploring every part of her body. "Remember when you were standing in your bedroom and I suddenly saw you through the mirror?" she asked suddenly.

"Do I. I'd already had enough temptation. It was a wonder I didn't come on the spot. You were straightening your seams. I wanted so much to stroke those legs, caress your pussy and smooth my hands over that lovely bottom." As I spoke, my hands were performing those actions. I kissed her pussy again, and let my hands continue stroking her bottom.

She gave Humphrey a few hard strokes which brought some of my juices onto her hand, licked them off and continued stroking it.

"What you didn't know was that I'd watched you over the years. You always left your light on when you were doing your exercises, or when you were reading or making models. I turned mine off and lay in bed watching you grow up. I saw your first erection, and then when you started to masturbate. That's when I first started employing au pair girls during, your holidays at home.

"I couldn't play with you then like I am doing now, but I thought having girls around would be a help. Had you forgotten them?"

I hadn't. The rough and tumble of school as a 13 year old, then back to the peace and tranquility of home. Mother had always found beautiful Scandinavian teenagers as au pairs. Their duties were not particularly onerous, the only real work was when I came home at half term, and then they had to care for me as well. But as Mother usually ate out, it meant sharing a spag bol, or an M and S special meal with me and perhaps a bottle of wine.

I was 13 or 14, they were 16 or 17. I was big for my age, so there wasn't much difference in size between us. They were in a strange country and lonely, I was at home and lonely. I gave, and received, a lot of comfort. Afterwards, we slept very well. It was my introduction to the joys of sex, and I was still in touch with several of my 'instructors'.

Mother laughed at the confusion on my face. "of course I knew. Did you think I would let just anybody introduce my son to the delights of the flesh? Do you remember your first time?"

"Ingrid, Inglit." "Inge" Mother corrected. "She was 17, you were 13, but you were ready, you were already playing with yourself." I blushed again, She laughed. "I told you, I was so proud of you, I used to study you, without you noticing of course. I met Inge when I was skiing in Italy. She was working as a chalet maid in the winter, but was looking for something to do in the Summer. I asked if she'd like to work for me, told her I had a teenage son who needed a bit of comfort. I'd already seen that she was an easy-going girl and guessed that things would take the normal course. And they did.

My mental video switched back to my first lay. It was a hot summer's day, I'd been lying by the pool we all shared in the flats, just swimming trunks on. Inge came down and saw me.

"Fancy a cold drink?" she asked, towel out alongside mine. There was would have liked better. "Lovely. I'll go."

"No, my idea" she answered. "I'll get them. Lime and soda?"

"Great."

I lay back on my towel, and minutes later felt the drops of ice-cold water on my crutch. I jumped up.

Of course, it was Inge, giggling at my reaction. "Ooh" she said. "I thought you were going to hit me, you were so angry.

I had been, but no longer, "Sorry" I said. "You have to be quick at school, it's the sort of thing they do there."

"The bullies" she said, putting the glasses down beside the towels. "They wouldn't do that if I was there." As she said it, she undid the bra of her bikini, dropped it beside the glass, and then ran her hands up the back of her hair, fluffing it out. Her breasts transfixed my eyes. I hadn't yet joined the big boys at school, so girls bodies were confined to glimpses of them dashing between gymnasium or sports field and changing rooms.

Inge sat down casually on her towel, picked up her glass, waited as I tore my eyes away from her figure to pick up my own. "Prosit" she said, and clinked glasses with me. My throat had gone completely dry, the cold lime and soda rejuvenated it. "Prosit" I responded, my eyes still trying to absorb the details of the vision lying next to me. I was now lying on my side, trying to appear casual whilst peering at her breasts through the gaps of the fingers clasped in front of my face.

Her attempts to start conversation failed dismally until, eventually, Inge took the bull by the horns, in a manner of speaking.

"Tony!" she called in a commanding voice. "Tony, take your hands away from your face and look at me. Have you never seen a naked girl before? Seriously. Have you?"

I was cornered. I shook my head.

"You mean you've never seen a girl without any clothes on, not even me."

I'd recovered the use of my voice. "No."

She seemed amazed. "Not even a girl servant, an auntie, your mother even?" "No" I answered even more emphatically. The very idea of seeing Mother in the nude was worse than sacrilege. Mothers NEVER took their clothes off, except for special occasions like holidays.

Mother had chosen well. Even at 17, Inge was a child psychologist. "We have to do something about that" she said, putting on her bra and picking up her glass and towel. "Come on" she ordered, and led the way to her room. I had never seen it before, though I could have inspected it at any time.

The reason why Mother never had trouble in getting, and keeping an au pair was clear. It was furnished in the same way as mine, perfectly comfortable for a couple never mind one person.

Inge took the glass and towel from me and motioned me to the bed. "Sit there" she commanded. I obeyed. "Right, you're 13, an adult and though you've never seen me naked, I've seen you dozens of times." I was about to protest, but she cut me short. "Every night, before I go to bed, I come into your room whether your mother is here or not, and check you are O.K. I pull down your duvet, sometimes I have to sort out your pyjama trousers, you do tie them in a knot. Sometimes I play with your penis - I know you do and maybe I give you a nice dream as I stroke it. Take your trunks off."

I obeyed, without really thinking, and sat on her bed. She paused only to undo her bra and drop her bikini bottom, before sitting beside me on the bed.

"Now you can look at me" she said, "and I'll look at you."

Even now, when I've seen so many breasts, kissed them, and kissed the pussies beneath them, I still remember that pair. Inge pulled my face across to her bosom, allowing me free reign with my tongue and lips on her nipples, while at the same time toying with my prick. Every boy should have the initiation she gave me. It was dusk, the lime and soda had long since gone when she turned my face to give me a kiss that meant something special.

"Tony, that was lovely. You have lovely big penis now you know everything I know."

It was a wonderful summer. Mother took us for a month to the villa Father owned in Portugal. She met him, it seemed, but Inge and I were left to our own devices. We acquired wonderful suntans. Yes, I remembered Inge. We still wrote.

"We're still in touch" I said. "She taught me a lot." Though I tried to keep my face straight, I couldn't help a half-smile turning the corners of my lips.

Mother laughed at my conceit. "She tells me. I had a letter from her last week, she's in London with her boss for some conference. Even wondered if she could have a refresher course from you. And she was your first. You must have impressed her, still recalling it three years later. I think I'll have to write back, now I'm taking care of that department, and say there are no vacancies ...unless there are things we could learn from the Continent?"

It was a big question Mother was asking, but it was hardly likely that we were going to be celibate during my absences at school, or rather that I was going to be celibate.

"Why not. She's one of the family anyway."

Years later, I realised that answer set the ground rules for our relationship. It gave us both sexual freedom when apart. No questions asked.

"Were you watching in those days, when Inge was teaching me?" I asked.

It wouldn't have been right. I couldn't have looked Inge in the face as she was serving us at the table if I'd been spying on you, though I did notice how often her breasts leant on your shoulders as she served your soup, and the way your hand slipped back to stroke her thigh."

"And I thought I was being so discreet." I giggled.

"You were actually. It was only because I was being so observant that I noticed these things. How many panties of hers' have you got?"

Typical Mother. Pop the big question in before they expect it, and then get a truthful answer.

"Only one. But it's dry now. If she comes down again I'll get it moistened."

"Pig" said Mother, digging me in the ribs so that I fell back. She gripped Humphrey and squeezed it. "Inge wanted to know if it was still as big. She knew it much better than me, I'd always been afraid to take your bedclothes off once you were in your teens. Inge loved it. She used to demonstrate how big it was with her hands, like a fisherman showing the fish he'd just caught, or lost.

"I'd no idea how big it was until you were standing in your bedroom and it was standing straight up. It was the biggest one I'd ever seen." She thought about what she'd said. "I haven't seen that many, honest."

"But when you were standing there, drying your back with that big thing sticking up. It was so big, I already felt sexy, what with you seeing me nude in the bathroom, then putting on my stockings, and then you and your towel, and there was I in undies. I wanted to hold that cock in my hand and then play with it in my mouth."

"It only needed one gesture and I would have been with you. When I saw you in the shower I was rampant. In fact I haven't stopped since. Stop talking. I want to kiss your pussy."

"Not as much as I want to kiss that fantastic cock. It's beautiful."

I had no idea that there was anything special about my private parts. True, I had no difficulty in getting girls, usually the best, to come to bed, but I thought it was all down to my innate charm, not the size of my weapon. Being a realist, I metaphorically shrugged my shoulders and enjoyed what I'd got.

It was time. I pulled Mother up from where she was lying on my thigh, my penis in her mouth. Had it not been so big, I'm sure she would have gone to sleep, but she was quick to respond when I touched her. She was as ready as I.

In Egypt and Rome, brothers married mothers and sisters. There was nothing strange in what we were about to do.

I moved a pillow under her buttocks, something I'd learned at school, it gave Humphrey deeper penetration. Then as I moved over her, she opened her legs and guided me into her pussy with both hands. I wanted it badly, and drove into her, screwing her as hard as I'd ever screwed anybody. She orgasmed within minutes, then broke down, crying bitter tears on my shoulder. "I'm sorry, I'm sorry. I'm, sorry" she sobbed. "I've spoilt it."

I was bemused, and so was Humphrey. I took her by the shoulders and pushed her away from me. "Stop crying. What's wrong?"

" I came too early." She took Humphrey in her hand, weighed it and stroked it. "And you're not anywhere near ready. I did so want our first to be fantastic."

I pulled her down beside me, letting her play with Humphrey. I gave her tits a squeeze and kiss.

"Listen, little lady. It's time I told you about the birds and the bees."

"And you learned all that at school?" she said in wonderment. "Even the little details."

"Even the little details. They don't actually say 'Now go out and practice', but it's just like watching a porno video.

"We're all randy, so it's out in the school grounds and knickers down. Even the teacher joins in."

I wondered whether I'd gone too far mentioning Miss Ellis, the teacher in charge of sex instruction. Any pupils leaving school without an expert knowledge of sex during the Miss Ellis reign had to have been deaf and blind. She believed in leading from the front on any natural history/biology/sex education expedition.

As soon as we were out of sight of the coach, she was stripped down to her shorts, her other clothes stuffed in her rucksack. Her example was followed immediately. Boots, socks and shorts were all that anyone wore on Miss Ellis' expeditions. Nettle stings on boobs or buttocks were disregarded.

We learned a lot about natural history, we learned much about biology and we all got A1 grades in sex education. "And that" I said, bending over so that I could kiss her clitoris, leaving her to toy with my prick as it dangled in front of her face, "is why a gentleman always makes sure that his lady has had her orgasm before he thinks about himself. There are so many ways she can give him pleasure."

Mother was learning fast. She lay back, taking Humphrey in both her hands and adjusted herself so that she was lying beside it.

"Let me try this way first" she said, and began licking its tip. I relaxed at once and let her have her way. She moved herself so that she could give it greater attention, and made herself available to my questing fingers. She sighed as my fingers found their way into her slit and began stroking her clit. She was a pagan on my prick, slurping her way round it, in and out of her mouth until her fingers felt the response. She re-doubled her efforts until my shout of pleasure was matched by her shout of joy as it gushed forth. There was so much it overflowed over her mouth. She rubbed it into her face, her boobs and her arms. She shrieked her delight. "Our first, Tony. Our first come. Isn't it wonderful?"

Chapter Three : Body Painting for Two

The incessant noise of the telephone woke me. It took me a second to recollect what had happened. There was no trace of Mother in the bed, and by the noise the phone was making, she wasn't in the flat either. I went into her bedroom, the party-goers had gone, and picked the phone up.

"Hallo" I rasped.

"Not feeling too good are we?" came the cheerful voice of Daphne. "Too much of one thing or the other? Now listen Sweetie Pie. I happen to know, 'cos your mother rang to tell me, that she's got some people coming round to tidy up the flat. So why don't you have a bath, get the old aerobics outfit on, that's the party theme, put a toothbrush in your pocket and jump into the Jaguar that'll be at your front door in thirty minutes. You might even have time for a coffee. Toodle pip." The phone went dead.

I looked around, the sitting room was empty of people, but filled with party remnants. I put the kettle on and ran a bath. Back in my room I saw the note on her pillow on my bed.

"Got to have a think. I've gone for a drive. See you when I get back. Don't worry. You'll get a phone call" was all it said.

Two blasts on the car's horn signalled the arrival of George and his car. I hadn't realised I was its last call. The half-dozen young ladies in leotards, bodies or just shirts and shorts were clapping and singing 'Why are we waiting' as I left the lift, and ran down to the car.

Four of them I hadn't met before, but two were my companions in yesterday's drive, Anita and Diana. I eased myself between them as they called out various names to me. Introductions over, I put an arm round each. They tensed, expecting me to take some form of revenge. Instead I kissed their ears. "Thank you for having me to your party" said Anita. The last time I'd seen her she was groping and being groped by a yuppie.

"I'm glad you came" I replied straight faced. "So am I" she murmured equally seriously and spoiled it by letting a big grin steal over her face. Without bothering to conceal her action she put her hand on my crutch, found Humphrey and gave him a big squeeze.

"If you get time" she giggled, "I've got a situation you could fit very fully. I'd like you to go into it more deeply."

"Not sure what today's programme is" I replied, "but rest assured that I'll do my best to bring matters to a happy conclusion, if not today, the very near future."

She chuckled. I cupped a breast through her shirt. I loved her sense of humour.

The ever-ready George was first out of the car and opened the side door to what was a block of offices in the centre of town. As we debussed, I murmured to Anita, "How do we make contact?"

"Anyway you like, but" she pushed a piece of paper into my trouser pocket, "my phone number's there." George ushered us into the lift and pressed the button for the penthouse.

That we learned was his, and Mrs George's last duty of the weekend. At the door of the penthouse we were greeted by the Double Dees, both in brightly coloured leotards and panties.

A kiss all round and we followed them through a large sitting room into the swimming pool. We spread ourselves around the edge of the pool as a slimly built aerobics teacher took up position by the diving board. "Can you hear me?" she called.

We could. The acoustics of swimming pools are designed to carry any whisper anywhere. It had caused me some problems in the past.

"Right, now all line up, that's right, those at the back, come forward a bit, a bit more, Perfect. Now follow me."

I had never liked the music from Grease. To hear "The one that I want, ha ha ha" and watching people jumping up and down to it was too much. I crept away.

Daphne met me at the door. "Guessed you wouldn't last long" she said. "Fancy a beer'?"

There was nothing I'd rather have seen at that moment. "You smooth talker. Where is it?"

"Follow me."

I did. I knew it had to happen some time or other. She certainly had me down for the fatted calf role, but who was I to refuse. I followed her up a spiral staircase and was thus able to study the pattern on her leotard. I was goggle-eyed at what I saw.

At the top I took a pace back to examine it more closely. It was the most erotic costume I'd ever seen, "Bet you've never seen an outfit like it. It's unique." she said.

She took me by the hand and led me to the windows of her suite. It wasn't really a flat, it was a suite of rooms similar to a hotel. It took up a corner of the penthouse. The walls were glass on both sides with balconies outside. The view was right over London. Spectacular.

"Dolores has the other half" she explained.

"Fantastic" I said, as I paced around the windows, the view changing constantly.

I was still intrigued by her erotic costume and led her to the light. It was of a Bacchanalian orgy, in the style of Aubrey Beardsley, little Satyrs holding enormous penises in front of them, chasing tall damsels who held their dresses up above their waists so that they could run more quickly, down her body until the last foot disappeared into her panties, the tip of a giant penis following leaving the frustrated satyr outside.

A snake, every woman's enemy, wound its way round each of her breasts, its head her nipple, jutting out, with eyes, mouth and fangs gleaming.

I moved around behind her. The scene continued at the back with the addition of a serpent which wound its way down her spine to lose itself in the panties she wore over the leotard.

I went back to her nipples. The detail of the snake's head was too exact to be cloth, whether nylon or cotton. I grasped them. There was no material.

My hands ran all over her body, her breasts, her bottom, her legs, all were naked. The only bit of clothing were her panties. It was a body painting. Daphne laughed. "Fooled everyone, didn't we?"

I clapped my hands in admiration. "Its beautiful. Dolores got the same?"

"Of course." I ran my hands over her, it was so realistic. She slipped out of her panties and put them in my pocket, whispering "For your pillow."

Even the patch underneath was painted, and the back showed where the serpent's head went, not to mention the painted ladies and satyrs. It must have been pretty crowded in there. I laughed and caressed it, then bent down to kiss that spot. She turned so I could kiss the front.

"I was going to have my pubes shaved off, needn't have worn anything then, but I know a girl who had hers' shaved for an operation. When they grew back they were so bristly, fellows didn't want to go down on her."

She led me to her bed and undressed me. There was no pretence and no false modesty. Humphrey was at his best. I'd missed some morning glory with Mother, and I was ready now.

I sat on her stomach while she rubbed Humphrey between her breasts, giving it the occasional kiss as it reached her lips.

"How long did it take to paint?" I asked. "Several hours. They came round early this morning, a couple from Goldsmiths' College. Dolores had the girl, the boy did me. I told him that if he was going to see me naked, he'd have to take his clothes off too." She giggled.

"Then what happened?"

"The inevitable. His erection kept getting in the way. There was only one thing for it. But don't worry, there's plenty left."

She moved from under me, still holding on to Humphrey. Her legs lifted and came round so that they were round my waist. She guided Humphrey into her, then crossed her feet behind me and with her legs pulling against my back, pulled me deep inside her. "Just a quick one now. We'll have a real one later."

I did as she asked.

We dressed, straightened the bedclothes and returned to the sitting room part of her suite. She pressed a button in the wall, and part of the wall slid back on itself to reveal Dolores' suite which had been given over to the buffet.

"That's fine. Now lets go for a swim."

She stopped me as I reached for my shorts and shirt. "You needn't think you're going to put some clothes on while I'm wandering around in the altogether. Everyone will be skinny-dipping. Just stick them in my wardrobe. You can always wear my knickers to go home in."

She was right. At the pool, boobs were jutting and penises dangling everywhere. Some were sitting tentatively on the sides of the pool, uncertain whether to go in the water. One of the few not to have stripped was the aerobics teacher.

Daphne gestured to her, "Get her to join in, she's here for the weekend too."

As she dived into the pool I watched to see if the paint was coming off. It wasn't, neither was that on Dolores who had joined her sister. They saw me looking and posed, arms outstretched, breasts prominent.

I'm sure the idea occurred to all three of us at the same time. They looked at each other, back to me and winked. I winked back.

The others were just realising that neither had a costume and there was mass groping as the body paintings were inspected.

I sauntered over to the teacher. She watched my advance with interest. Her eyes had taken in my nudity. "Don't you swim?" I asked.

"Well, yes, but I'm not really a guest." That was O.K. She could swim.

"Of course you're a guest" I said and bent down to pick her up. She was struggling as I held her in my arms and then jumped into the water.

"You're a pig" she shouted to me, after coming to the surface. She grabbed the side of the pool and was trying to climb out when I stopped her by grabbing the waistband of her tracksuit bottoms, quickly unzipping the ankles and pulling the trousers off. I threw them into the pool where they were grabbed by some of the boys who were cheering my efforts.

She gave up trying to climb out, instead turning and falling on me, sending me down to the bottom. She had taken a deep breath, I hadn't and was soon gasping for air. I struggled to rise, but she kept me down by the simple expedient of holding my cock. I'd begun to panic when she let me go. At the surface, I gulped in air and held onto the pool rail. The tug on my cock took me by surprise, and I almost lost my grip. She surfaced beside me, grinning.

"If you can't beat them, I suppose you'd better join them" she said, and trod water whilst pulling her tracksuit top over her head. I gave her a hand, gripping the rail firmly with one hand as I helped her disrobe. I made no pretence at hiding my inspection of her breasts, small as one would expect of an aerobics teacher, but firm.

"Will they pass muster?"

"You know they do, but what about those?"

I looked down through the water to her legs. At their join was a pair of satin briefs, nothing glamorous but certainly fanciable.

"In for a penny..." she shrugged, "but you can do the honours."

It meant going under water with her above me, and risking being held under again, but I couldn't back out. I took a deep breath and went under. As I crooked a finger on each side of her briefs she reminded me of how powerless I was, by holding my head under for a second. Then she raised her legs and bent them, so that stripping them took only mini-seconds. I tied them to the pool rail and hoped no-one else would find them.

"You've got an erection!" she said, her turn to look down into the water. She was quite right. Its tip was rubbing against her stomach. She was leaning against the pool-side, facing me.

"How did that happen?" all innocence.

"Probably because of the attention it's been getting from you."

"Will it go away?"

"Not until after."

"After what?"

For answer, I bent down, lifting her buttocks up so that I was standing, her legs on either side of me and Humphrey perfectly positioned.

"After this" I answered.

She tried to move. "You can't do it here" she protested.

"I already am." I answered. It was true. Humphrey had found his own way in, helped by the warm water and, perhaps, the muscles in her pussy. I had a quick glance round, no-one was taking any notice of us, they were all occupied. Some had already gone up the spiral stairs to the buffet. I set up a steady rhythm.

"What about your girlfriend. You ARE with Daphne?"

"Yes. But I'll see to her later. By the way, is she a friend of yours"?"

By then, she had abandoned herself to the pleasures she was getting. Her legs had tightened around me, if I'd wanted to break away I couldn't.

"I was the P.E. teacher at the school they've just left. They knew I was newly qualified, didn't know many people and asked if I'd take a class or two at the weekend."

"Well, it is one way of getting to know people" I said dryly, giving her an extra hard push. I seemed to be cornering the market in P.E. teachers.

She gave my bum a pinch.

"Will you see to me later. A real seeing to I mean. I've got some surprises in store for you."

"What sort of surprises?"

"I'll show you later."

She untied her legs from my waist, and pushed me away from her. Humphrey, reluctantly, floated to the surface.

"Let's have something to eat." she said. I don't want you coming just yet, and I don't suppose any of the other girls here do either. I've already had one or two dirty looks."

Hands on the side of the pool, a dolphin type leap and she was out of the water, standing on the side in one movement. I wondered how it was that I'd managed to capture her so easily.

I remembered the briefs, concealed them in my hand and accepted the hand she offered to pull me out of the water. We collected her track-suit and hung it to dry on the backs of some chairs.

There was a pile of towels in the changing room. I dried her, she dried me.

Chapter Four : The Double-double Dees

There was a touch of the Nero party about the scene in the Double Dee's suites of rooms. The only garments being worn were towels draped as togas, and not too many of them. The twins dominated the rooms, moving tableaux as guests studied their paintings. Somehow they didn't look nude, and though they were unclothed, shapely long legs, Junoesque breasts, their figures didn't excite as they would have done normally.

Dolores had St George and the Dragon writhing all round her, the dragon holding a naked girl captive while St George, wearing only frontal armour, every muscle in his rear isolated, was about to impale the dragon's mouth - her navel - with his sword.

My first move was to hide the briefs, embroidered with an 'E' for Erika, in my shorts, then I could rejoin the group.

I had just done so when I was clasped from behind I didn't need to know whose hands they were, one went straight to my groin and found Humphrey. Then Dolores, was lifting my legs, and they carried me to the bed. "What were you thinking as you saw us together in the pool?" asked Daphne.

"The same as you two I expect" I replied. "The three of us have got the same vibes. I could see myself between your breasts, kissing one pair then the other, one hand on each of your pussies, then kissing one and letting

Humphrey have his way with the other. What was it you visualised?"

"Much the same" said Daphne, snuggling down beside me so that her breasts were pressing against one side of my face, those of Dolores on the other, "but we have got some variations we'll try one day."

As if I'd left out something, they each took my nearest hand and placed it on their fannies. My fingers automatically took up position, three playing inside the lips of the labia, the thumb placed firmly on the clitoris.

As usual, Daphne was first to break the role, climbing over so that she had straddled my thighs, and was already moving Humphrey inside her. I was too occupied to see Dolores move, though I felt the oil being brushed over the fingers of first Daphne's hands and then my own. I felt Dolores turn onto her front, a hand reaching out for mine. She pulled it onto her fanny and began using my hand to massage herself. Then I found my fingers being used to massage another area altogether. Her little bumhole opened as my finger touched it, and at the same moment, I felt a finger touching mine.

I kept perfectly still. Despite the attempt at the farewell party, this was a new experience for me. Soft, creamy fingers were gently moving between the cheeks of my bottom, and then moving into the little hole.

"Now me" Daphne whispered into my ear.

Her thighs lifted higher, gripping my waist even more tightly as my hand slid underneath them. I didn't really need any oil, her own juices were enough to open the little hole which grew bigger as my finger and then fingers began their massage.

Dolores moved up so that she was lying parallel, but face down, with her sister. She took my free hand, and placed it on her bottom, massaging her cheeks with it until she moved it down to the cleft between her thighs, which opened wide. I freed my hand and cupped everything there for a few seconds, before complying with what I knew she wanted. First one finger, then two began their exploration of her bottom.

Daphne had grown still, as if knowing that her sister was being pleasured, even though she still kept a gentle movement in and out of my bottom, her fingers going in deeper each time.

Then, as if at a signal, she moved to her right so that I found myself sliding onto Dolores. As I did so, her bottom lifted into the all-fours position. Her hand guided it to the little button.

"I want to feel it in there" said Dolores. "But take it very slowly. Ah, that's it."

I felt her sphincter muscles expand as Humphrey's tip opened them. From beneath me came a gasp of exultation.

"Feels beautiful. Ever since I first saw it in the changing room, and sat on it in the car, I've wanted it just here. Push a little bit."

I did, and felt another inch of Humphrey slide in, to deep sighs from Dolores. Daphne's fingers meanwhile were continuing their own exploration and were easing in and out of my rear.

I began to pump, feeling a tightness around it that no other pussy could imitate. Humphrey was gripped in a vice for the first half of its length.

Beneath me, Dolores had picked up my rhythm.

"Now. she urged, push it all in, ram it in me."

" Aaargh, oaargh!!." It was almost a scream which brought Daphne round to her. Dolores collapsed onto her front, leaving Humphrey dangling and me feeling like some monster.

Daphne was muttering words like "Are you hurt",

"Shall we get an ambulance" when Dolores lifted her face up. She turned over, but lowered her bottom very gingerly on the bed and reached forward to grasp me and give me a smacking kiss.

Humphrey had been so surprised by events that he had retreated into his shell.

Dolores reached a hand into my loins to bring him out. "As far as I'm concerned, that's it" she said, stroking him and bringing him back to life. I've had lots of fingers playing with me there, and I've wondered what it would be like. Now I know. It was wonderful, fantastic, amazing. I thought I could come for ever, but I know it will never happen like that again. Now I'm going to have a nice long bath, and put a cushion under me."

She muttered a few words to Daphne, gathered a towel round her and went towards her own suite.

"What did she say?" I asked. "Have I hurt her." Daphne paused before answering. "No-o. She's a bit sore, but she knew that would happen. What she said was that if I wanted to try it with you, tonight was the night. We would never have another opportunity."

"Why not?"

"It doesn't really matter, you great muffin" she said, flinging her arms round me, and rubbing her breasts against my chest. "Would you like to take me like that?"

"Not if it caused you pain. You and Dolores have a sort of code I don't know about. If she told you not to chance it, then that's it."

"Ah, but she didn't. She said it was the best fuck she's ever had, or ever likely to have, because she couldn't go through with it again."

"You mean it was that painful and...."

"Yes. It was a once for all time experience. And, Yes, I want it."

As I went to the bathroom for a quick washdown, she pressed a button. Part of a wall slid across to divide her bedroom from the party-goers in the sitting room.

Another button swung open a section of a wall to reveal a bar. I couldn't help being impressed.

"Bravo."

She grinned. "I adore you. You're always so natural. You never pretend."

"Why should I?"

"Never mind. Would you like something? It's got everything. Don't know why, until now, I've never wanted to open it."

"Lime and soda?" I asked.

"I'm sure we've got that" and she busied herself in her bar. Two minutes later, "Whisky and soda?"

I held my arms out to her and she threw herself into them, rubbing her painted body all over me.

Our caresses moved from one level to a higher one. My hands exploring her all over, her hands exploring mine. I was kissing her clitoris, one finger stroking in and out of her bumhole while she had a finger in mine, when she said : "Let's do it."

It was difficult, but I had to say it, "Dolores had been practising much longer than you. It was nowhere near as tight."

"In that case" said Daphne reaching out for the bottle of oil, "as I love you more anyway, I'll have a much better fuck than her, and so will you because you love me more than her. Correct." I nodded.

"All it means my darling, is that you'll have to be that much more gentle, that much more innovative, that much more loving."

She poured small quantities of the oil on my hands and then her own. Hers' went immediately to Humphrey. I massaged her waist. I didn't like the taste of baby oil, and it was only later when I brushed the sweat from my face that I realised it was real olive oil. Until then, I kept it away from her pussy and her little button.

We had enjoyed so much sexual activity that day that it was only the thought of forbidden territories that kept us both alert. I increased the pressure on Daphne, knowing that if I didn't, she would get disheartened. With Dolores there had been competition. Daphne understood it as well as I.

"I want it. I know we're not white hot, but I'm red hot. Once you're inside, you'll be white hot." She went into the doggy position, and pulled Humphrey towards her. I smoothed her pussy towards her button, and let the juices mingle before venturing first one, and then as it became accepted, a second, inside. As I moved them in and out, I could feel Daphne responding, her bottom moving in sympathy.

I thrust a little bit, helped by Daphne's hand which came up to clasp Humphrey. Her bottom moved backwards as she thrust him forward onto her. She would have continued pushing but I stopped, and let her muscles get adjusted to this intruder which was now half inside her.

"Tony?" I bent over to her. "Can you feel it? It's so smooth. I want it all now darling. Squeeze my breasts, push a bit more, moRE. *MORE*. NOW. LOVELY, *LOVELY*, DRIVE IT IN. THAT'S IT. *OOHH!!*. KEEP ON FUCKING ME, AGAIN, *AGAIN,* **AGAIN**,"

I drove into her at each demand even though I knew I was hurting her. She told me later she came at least three times, but reiterated the point Dolores had made, she would never want to do it again.

It was time to rest. "Darling, do me a favor. Leave me. I just want to rest. If I don't come down when everyone's going, see them out and then come up here - if you want to. O.K."

"Not yet. How long has this paint been on?"

"Since about six o'clock this morning"

"And its about what now, four o'clock?" "Half past" said Daphne looking at her Rolex. "Don't say you're worried about us?"

"Of course I'm worried. How do you think I could explain to Helen that I'd been to a party at which her cousins had died?"

` I ducked as Daphne pretended to strike me. "You-u-u wait" she threatened.

"Seriously" I continued. "I think it's time it came off. I know it blocks up your pores and suffocates you. Apart from that it looks as if you're wearing clothes. You look much sexier without it."

I couldn't have found a better argument. "We've got some cream and lots of cotton wool. You can help us wipe it off."

"No need for you to do anything" I replied. "Get the cream and the cotton wool."

While she went to get it, I went into Dolores bedroom. She was fast asleep, but I had no compunction in shaking her awake. At first she hated me, but when I explained my worry, she understood, particularly when she learned how she was going to be bathed.

We collected towels and stretched them out on the floor. Dolores was already in position sitting cross-legged when her twin returned.

"Right fellers" I called to the others as they sat talking or snogging. Give me a hand to get this paint off these ladies.

As the hands groped them, the girls took the easy way out, lay down and closed their eyes. Not a corner of their anatomy was missed. Dolores said she could have come a dozen times with the amount of massaging her nipples and clitoris got. "Didn't want to spoil it for them by saying there was no paint there" she said. "Anyway I was enjoying it."

White once again, they went for a shower, and a touch of make-up. Dolores went to a TV set in the corner and inserted a tape in the video.

"Porno" she said, "for the benefit of those who only want to watch."

"That gives me an idea" said Dolores. She was gone for several minutes, then led me into her bedroom. "Had to get some pictures off the walls" she said, pressing another button in the wall, part of which slid back behind us, cutting off the bedroom completely. "Didn't want people coming in to watch us, did we."

Another button drew lightproof curtains over the glass walls. A gentle glow of light came from the ceiling. I lay beside her, a hand on a nipple. Her hands began caressing me.

I squeezed the nipples, kissed them, ran my tongue all round her breasts and gave her a deep kiss as I cupped her pussy.

I slid to the end of the bed so that I could lift her buttocks and bring her pussy to my face. Dolores slid down with me. As I was burying my face in her quim I felt her underneath me, taking my penis into her mouth.

She put Humphrey to one side of her face, rubbing him against her cheek. "Was everything O.K.?" she asked.

"Perfect" I answered. "She's having a little sleep now, but I think she'll be up shortly." "Did she like it?" Dolores put the question brutally.

"I think so, though she said, like you, that she wouldn't do it again. Would you?"

It wasn't a question Dolores had expected.

"Remember how it all started? It was only today. It was before we got really serious. Daphne was on top of me and you wanted some as well. "I want it too," you were shouting.

"So I climbed on you and you bucked me like the rider in a rodeo, your knees gripping my waist. Then you rolled so that we were side by side, your legs gripping me.

"Squeeze my tit," you demanded. My right hand was almost pinned by a leg, but I managed to manoeuvre it to that I could grip a nipple. My left hand was already squeezing a right nipple. I turned my hand over so that my thumb, instead of being underneath was on top, giving me an extra half turn of your nipple. That and an extra hard squeeze made all the difference.

"The pair of you were screaming as if someone had stolen your ice cream." I admonished. Daphne had crept in and burbling with delight as she disentangled herself so that she could get her mouth to Humphrey. First Daphne, then Dolores, then together, they gave him real birthday treatment. He was bounced from one mouth to another, from one pair of breasts to another, from one juicy, damp pussy to another. Daphne left Dolores to work on his cock while she concentrated on his bottom. It opened quite easily under the influence of her tongue,

"Do you like it?" she asked. "Not sure, it's different."

As she began moving her hand up and down, I reached my hand down to her pussy, made my fingers wet and began playing with her bottom. My fingers slipped in easily, and as I massaged her she uttered soft little moans.

I left my fingers in there. "Did you really want it this afternoon?"

She held me to her, stroking me and caressing me everywhere except my groin.

"A boyfriend liked to do it to me while I did it to him. As he came, I pushed it right up him, then dragged it out and he'd do the same when I came. It was the best we knew about sex. But then we met Helen, learned about your school, met you and some of the other pupils. Wonderful."

"Would you like it now in your pussy?"

"Yes", she breathed. "I'm ready anyway."

"Which is the best way? You or me on top?"

"You on top. Reach over to that bedside cabinet, see that bottle, right take the tap off and pour some over me."

I got the distinctive smell of olive oil. She rubbed it into Humphrey, then around her pussy, her bottom and then mine. Humphrey didn't need any help to go into her. I was just stroking her lovely bottom, avoiding the parts of her that I knew were painful, when she held my fingers and took my hand down to her bottom. My fingers slipped in easily. She teased mine open again and began to play with it.

Our strokes synchronised. I knew I was coming, and she could feel the tension in my prick through her pussy.

"You go for it" she whispered, "I'll be able to come after."

I reached my climax and spurted everything into her, feeling the added excitement as she pushed her finger right up and then snatched it out. I continued pumping, but she had gone off the boil once I'd come." "No more for me for the moment" she said and pulled my hand away.

"Did you like it?"

"Yes, but I'm not sure it's a good idea. What happened to that boyfriend?"

Daphne laughed. "He got to like it so much he was doing it with boys, but not with fingers."

Chapter Five : Backbend with a Difference

It was a relief to hear that because of the problems our opponents had in finding a team for today's match, they would like to postpone it. The Captain had found out where I was from Helen - who had not been invited, and who undoubtedly would be peeved. Four leading members of the team, myself included, received the news with gratitude.

As it was Sunday, I tied a towel around my waist before going in search of coffee. Erika had been flexible, she was already in the kitchen, breasts jutting, with the arm of my rival from the 2nd team around her. He gave me a smug smile. "Coffee?" she asked. I nodded, and she brought down another cup. The coffee was already percolating, and the aroma attracted a wider audience. She laughed, poured out three cups and handed one to me. "First come, first served" she called, and made way for the rush.

As she left, with her new companion in attendance, she called out a number to me. I waited till they'd gone before finding a piece of kitchen paper and a pen to write it down.

A weekend orgy never quite lives up to its promise. By the second day, boys, and girls, if they'd been working at it, were jaded and desperately looking for a bed in a darkened room. As I fumbled for my shirt and shorts in Daphne's wardrobe, I heard her stir.

"Is that you?" she asked, and opened an eye to see that it was. Reassured, she added,

"You going?"

"Yes." I said, bending over to kiss her. "We've done it all for the time being. The Double Dees have been the most wonderful hostesses and I've made so much wonderful love to them that if I'm castrated tonight, I'll have enough memories to last me." I brought us down to reality by adding, "I need a kip, you must fancy a bit of sleep too."

She pulled my face down for a long, lingering kiss. "You're such a wise, wonderful lover. In ten years time we could make a wonderful match. I'll ring you in the week."

I saw the phone in the sitting room and rang home. There was no reply. I tried again in case I'd misdialled. Still no reply. Mother had obviously decided to go away for the weekend as well.

When I turned, Erika was sitting by herself, wearing her tracksuit. My rival, from the second team, who hoped that I would break a leg, so he could replace me, had gone.

"I saw you were getting dressed, which meant you weren't staying here, so I sent him off."

"Good" I said. "Now we can have lunch at my flat."

"Fine, but can I have my briefs back for a while, its chilly outside."

I felt for them in my shorts pockets. Hers' were a satiny material whereas those of the Double Dees were silk and lace. It wouldn't do to bring the wrong pair out.

The satin was unmistakeable. Like a conjuror bringing a rabbit from a hat, I produced them, kissed them and gave them back to her.

She played up to the occasion, taking her trousers off to reveal a naked pair of legs and pussy, and handing the briefs to me to put on.

"You may as well do the honours again." she said.

I knelt down, and with her supporting herself with a hand on my shoulder, slid them up her legs. I squeezed them against her pussy while she set them comfortably around her waist. The tracksuit bottoms went on the same way, with me doing up the zips at her ankles. I kissed her breasts thoroughly before allowing myself to cover them, with the track-suit top.

No-one was stirring. I'd already thanked the hostesses for their hospitality, and I didn't doubt that they would be just as generous in the future…

The money in her jacket was damp but valid, and bought us a cab ride back to my flat.

As Daphne had predicted, cleaners had been called and the flat was spotless. There was a message on the ansaphone, She had decided to spend a few days with Nancy.

Erika was inspecting the flat. "Which is your room?"

I took her by the wrist and led her through Mother's room to my own. I was about to leave her to it when I remembered the pillow. Had I put a pair there, if so, whose were they?

I'd no idea, but it was certain that left alone, Ingrid would be plumping the pillows up and..... Things were moving too fast, so fast I couldn't keep up with them. I needed some sort of social secretary to keep my affairs, unintended pun, in order.

"While I sort things out here," I said, "do you fancy making a couple of lime juices and soda, its all in the fridge. And I'll start sorting out some lunch." I waited until I was sure she was in the kitchen before looking under the pillow. I was right. That black, lacy garment of Mother's had materialised again. That one of Mother's went under my shirts in the wardrobe, those of the Double Dees were distributed into my trainers. Ingrid's briefs could now take pole position.

Her tracksuit was now so well trained that it almost came off by itself. My hands assisted it. She posed for me to take her briefs off which I placed beneath my pillow with some ceremony, after holding them against her pussy so that her juices dampened them, then pressing them to my lips.

In seconds my clothes were off - a tee shirt and shorts are the ideal seducer's outfit - but Humphrey was in need of action before he would show his true qualities. Ingrid was about to provide it.

She stood in the centre of the carpet, her back to me, her legs apart, then commanded:

"Sit down, keep your legs together and put them between mine so Humphrey is directly underneath me."

I complied, whereupon she bent her body backward so it was like a hula hoop, her wrists gripping her ankles and her face directly above my penis which she took in her mouth. Then she put her hands on the floor and brought her legs back so she was in a handstand, my penis still in her mouth. I could just imagine her arms losing their strength, her falling to the floor still with Humphrey gripped firmly in her mouth as her teeth came together.

Chapter Six : Togas Down

The nearby village was seldom visited by pupils. It offered nothing that they couldn't get at school, though the pupils offered much to the village youth of both sexes. Occasionally one group met the other, swimming in the river or the lake during a hot spell, or when fruit needed picking. But it wasn't as easy for the town to take advantage of gown as gown was of gown.

The biggest party of the year was that held traditionally when the sixth formers celebrated their departure either for university or careers in the stock exchange - work as the undergrads called it disparagingly. These 18 year olds, boys and girls, chose a theme for a Bacchanalian revel, decorated the library in keeping with the theme, and furnished it with cushions. While kept exclusive, the numbers were made up by inviting the members of the rugby, football and cricket teams from the boys, and the netball, hockey and swimming teams from the girls. I was in the rugby team and had been to last year's party, given by Nero. The costume could not have been more simple, a sheet worn as a toga.

The more voluptuous the girl, the smaller the sheet. I was one of the earliest arrivals as I had made an arrangement with Helen, one of my best supporters at the rugby match. She was 18, one of the leavers, and we had been an 'item' since getting it together at the last end of year party. I grabbed a couple of glasses of the fruit punch - it wasn't supposed to have alcohol in it, but I knew it did - and picked my way in the semi-darkness to the cushions in a corner. Helen didn't keep me waiting.

Normally she wore her hair in a pigtail, but this time it was let down, over her shoulders. She sank down beside me and took the glass of steaming punch I offered her. We had plenty of time, and waited until the glasses were almost empty before I pulled her over to me. A hand slipped between the folds of her sheet found her breasts, her nipples already hard. I massaged them gently feeling her interest grow as I did so. She undid the brooch at her shoulder so that the sheet fell off, showing her completely naked body.

I bent to kiss her breasts, her hand finding the gap in my own toga where my prick was already straining for attention. She pulled it out so that she could massage her thighs with it. My hand slid down her tummy, paused to explore her navel, and continued the journey until it was at her pussy. My fingers stroked inside, it was deliciously soft and wet. I lifted my head from her breasts to look at her face. She was beautiful. She felt the same as I did, and her arms encircled my neck to pull me down to her for a long, long kiss. She took my hand and put it on a breast then pushed my head down to the other one. Her hand returned to my cock and slowly she began to move the foreskin up and down, gripping it tightly, Then she slid away from me and turned so that she could take it in her mouth. She treated my cock like a giant lollipop, licking and sucking it.

It would have been so easy to come, but I wanted to last a long time that night. I moved her head away, and instead bent down over her thighs. I gently bit the sides, that soft, cool palace that guards the heat of her pussy, and then plunged my face and tongue into it. Her clitoris was already proud and it was easy to tease it with my lips and then my teeth, gently tugging it. I could feel Helen twitching, and hear her panting, but she wasn't ready to come. I turned round, knelt over her and waited for her to hold my cock and then guide it into her. So very, very smooth. I let it lie there, feeling the softness of her pussy as she tensed its muscles and squeezed my prick.

Then I felt fingers massaging my bottom.
choice, and definitely not while I was making love.

"What's wrong?" Helen asked from underneath me. "Someone was trying to fuck me" I answered. She giggled and her vagina squeezed my cock even more tightly.

"How funny. Did you let him?"

"No. I don't fancy being a rape victim."

"Good. I don't think I like the idea of you in bed with another man. I know girls do it, but it doesn't seem quite so bad somehow."

"I agree. I don't fancy the idea of some hairy-arsed fellow cuddling up against me either."

The edge had gone off our passion. We both felt it. Helen was the first to raise it.

"That's rather spoiled it for me" she said, giving me a little push so that I rolled off her. "Made it rather sordid."

"I know. Me too." I was already limp. It had slipped out and was lying, moist still, on Helen's thigh. She gave it a little pat.

"I fancied a really long fuck with you, but I've sort of had enough. Think I'll leave it for tonight." She pushed herself up into a sitting position, and pulled the sheet around her. She leaned over me, letting me kiss first one breast, then the other before planting a firm kiss on my lips. She got to her feet, pinned the ends of her toga together with the brooch, blew me a kiss, and was gone.

I reassembled my toga, retrieved our glasses, and picked my way over the couples to where the bowl of punch stood. I refilled my glass and stood sipping it, watching what was happening on the floor.

Had anyone asked, it would have been denied, but a number of the younger members of staff had joined the throng. There was no mistaking the gym mistress. She was a noted swimmer and looked very much like Sharron Davies, a resemblance emphasised by her normal costume, a black one piece swimsuit which concealed, yet displayed a wonderful pair of breasts, tracksuit bottoms and trainers. The advantages of her figure were hidden as she sat in her toga, surrounded by a group of adoring girls.

P.E. teachers always brought out the lesbian tendencies in teenaged girls, but I was convinced that Miss Cartwright wasn't butch. She always kept the girls at a distance, and was usually seen on her own. I'd often fantasised about pulling her swimsuit over her shoulders and nuzzling against her bosom. There wouldn't be a better opportunity, and in any case, why had she come to the end of year students' party if she didn't want to take part?

I wound my way on hands and knees over the other embracing couples until I was in a kneeling position behind her. There were gasps of outrage as I began massaging her shoulders, feeling the softness of those powerful shoulder muscles. She grasped my hands and turned to see who they belonged to. Satisfied, she turned back and let me continue. The gasps grew in intensity as my hands began massaging further and further inside the toga until they were cupping her breasts and nipples. Miss Cartwright made no attempt to stop me, but there was no more conversation with her acolytes, instead they began to drift away in disillusionment.

      She fell back onto the cushions, pulling me down on top of her. She undid the pin which held her garment together, and waited. I took the hint and pulled it apart. There were her breasts, a swimmer's breasts, big as Israeli melons. I buried my face in them, kissing every part I could, nibbling at her nipples in an ecstasy of lust. She put a hand on my head and pressed my face even harder into them.

      "You're a brave boy Tony" she said. "Bite them hard, harder, harder. There, that's lovely" as I brought my teeth together on a nipple. I had been so busy with her breasts that I had not examined the rest of her body. She pulled my head up and turned it towards her legs. There was so much of her to explore. I slid my hand down to where I expected to find knickers. There were none, just the soft down of a pussy. She took my hand and pushed it into its centre.

      "I wondered if anyone would be brave enough to approach me" she said. "I've wanted this for so long. I'm glad it was you that tried it. And if you want to know why I'm glad it is you, it's because I've heard my girls make comments about you. "And this" she slid her hand inside my toga drawing out my massively erect organ, "is what they talk about. No wonder."

She cuddled up close to me so that I was squashing her breasts and my prick was squashed between us. I slid a hand up between us so that I could toy with her nipples. They were as big as nutmegs. I felt little jerks of her thighs as I caressed them. She whispered into my ear, "There's a direct line from my right nipple to my clitoris. Squeeze it and I'm on my back with my legs in the air."

"I'm glad I discovered it." I whispered back. "Nobody else try it?"

"All those little girls hanging around me scared off most men. They thought I was Butch. How come you didn't? I couldn't really put up a sign saying I'm normal. All I could do was come to this party. I thought one of the staff would try a flirtation, but they all dodged me. Might be different after this evening though. So, what made you so bold?"

"Two things. You were either on your own, or with a crowd of girls, never with just one. Second, why come to a party like this if you were Butch? All you needed to do if you didn't want me to touch you was shrug me off. When you let me continue massaging your shoulders I knew I could be outrageous because you didn't want the little girls around you. That's why I went straight for your breasts."

"It certainly drove them off. And gave me a moist pussy. What are you going to do about it? According to the girls, you are the only boy who can take his pick of the girls. You certainly rate 10 on the wall of the girls' toilet. I've seen it."

She didn't wait for me to do something, she provided the answer to her question herself. One arm beneath me and I was moved over on top of her, her other hand guided my missile neatly into its bed.

Because of her usual tracksuit, I hadn't seen her legs, and I'd been too busy to pay much attention to them this time. They curled up around me as I began to shaft her. Even in their semi-relaxed state I could feel the power in her muscles. If she went full strength in her orgasm I could end up with broken ribs.

She must have been psychic. Without interrupting our rhythm she murmured to me, "You're the best lover I've had for years. You'll be even better in three years time. Then we'll really go for it."

She almost forgot her promise when she reached her crescendo. Her legs tightened, and I had fears for my next match as I felt my ribs creak, but then they relaxed. and she uttered a long sigh, her body shuddering as she came. She laughed and giggled like a schoolgirl, bringing my head down to her for a deep kiss. "I almost forgot" she gurgled. "I wanted to strain my legs against you, but I remembered your bones weren't hard yet. But that was lovely, fantastic. Now, what about you?"

"I've already had everything I've fantasised about" I answered. I had to see your breasts. I've ached to see them since you first came to the school, when I was 14.

And how old are you now, 16?

"And a bit" I laughed. "She laughed back, and gripping my cock tightly added, "its a big bit."

"Big enough?" I asked.

"Proved it today, though it'll probably mean I'll lose all my admirers for ever. You're still hard" she murmured, holding it in her hands. "Does that mean you want seconds?"

For answer, I moved on top of her, and felt her legs go round my waist again as she fed my cock into her pussy. It was still tight and it gripped the sides of me as I thrust into her. We took our time about it. "It's beautifully tight" I whispered. "And your's is beautifully big" she whispered back. "I haven't had a lot of practice recently, but" she dropped into a West Country accent, "Oi do know what I loike and I do like this, and you, my poppet, are going to fuck the arse off me. I want every drop of your juices to spurt up inside me, and if they don't I'll squeeze you out of action in rugby for the rest of the season."

She was a gorgeous lover. Out of practice she might have been, but she hadn't wasted her time in the past. As I came inside her, she held me, mothered me, squeezed me to her.

"Baby, baby, baby let it come" she murmured, the muscles in her quim gripping me so that no last drop of my juices were left. As I subsided, she bent over to lick the end of my weapon.

"Now, young man" she said, putting her hands on each side of my face, to lend emphasis to her words. "I will tell you, I've just played Russian Roulette with you. I've stopped taking the Pill, and you weren't using a condom. Perhaps I'll become pregnant. Will you be pleased?"

I knew how my father must have felt when Mother became pregnant with me. A father, me, at 16, I hadn't even left school.... the expressions must have chased themselves across my face as she watched them.

"I wasn't joking Tony, but I want you to remember this date just in case it does happen. "Don't worry, I've wanted a baby by some wonderful father, and when you started caressing me this evening I couldn't think of a better candidate.

"If I fall, everything is arranged. I have enough money to look after the child until he or she is a teenager. If nothing happens, I'll be back at school next year. We might even meet up at the next end of year party.

"By then the crowd of potential candidates to father a child for her would be enormous. I had to say something.

"Mother and father were 16 when I was born. I don't think Grandmother was much older when she had Mother. We've survived, and if we have a child I'll make sure it, and you survive. If you don't come back next year, where will you be?"

I'd got over the initial shock of possible fatherhood. She had read the expressions on my face. "You know, I bet you don't even know my first name. What a thing from the possible father of my child. It's Ingrid, and you don't know my age either. I'm 24."

Eight years. It wasn't such a big gap, and I couldn't imagine having a more glamorous or more sensual partner. I made up my mind. "Of course our baby will have a name", I said. "I'll be 17 by the time he's born, only another year and then I'll be able to go to work. If you can manage for that year everything will be fine."

She ruffled my hair. "Wonderful Tony, All these promises and you don't even know if you hit the spot.

"So where will you be? If I haven't hit it this time I can have another go. As you said, you're out of practice."

She giggled. I'll ring you tomorrow and give you my address. You won't remember it now, and you've got nothing to write on. Now I think I'd better go. I'm off to France at the weekend, but I'll ring you before I go. Come to lunch." Her mind already on departure, she looked around. "I wonder how many people have seen us."

Enough. Helen was one. I recognised her ankles and her ankle bracelet as they paused in passing us. I waited until she moved on before looking up from Ingrid's pussy. Helen was with a newly qualified maths teacher, Mr Cockin, known already to his pupils as 'Butcher'. I'm sure Helen was making sure he did. What was sauce for the goose....

"I don't think you'll have any shortage of company at next year's party - if you come back. But I'll still be here."

I leaned over her, taking first one, then the other magnificent breast in my mouth. The place was emptying. She gave my prick a squeeze and kiss, then a lingering kiss on the mouth.

"I'll ring you tomorrow. "You can take it from there." She uncurled herself from the floor, arranged her sheet to cover her, and was about to leave when I asked, "Have you got any panties?"

"Yes. Why?"

"Put them on."

Mystified, she opened a small bag I hadn't noticed, and produced a pair of white panties. First one long leg was revealed, then a second as she pulled them on. Covered, she turned, "Now what?"

For answer, I squeezed them against her pussy, felt them dampen, then bent down to kiss them.

"I want them to keep under my pillow. I've got nowhere to put them now but wear them on Wednesday. Don't wash them. I'll take them home afterwards."

"I see. I thought you were making sure no-one else enjoyed the privileges you've just been given."

"That too." I held her legs as she climbed to her feet and knelt up so that I could give her pussy a last kiss. I let the toga drop. She moved quietly away, ignoring the remaining acolytes who had watched events disapprovingly.

Some followed her, but she moved so fast they were left behind. One couple remained. There was a slight reverence as if I had been in touch with a goddess when one plucked up courage to ask, "What was it like?"
"Wonderful" I replied.

"Of course, it would be."

The girls were about the same age as the Double Dees, would probably be in their class at school, but the difference couldn't have been wider. They were the type who would have rushed to join the supporters of some American evangelist, naive innocents.

The girl spoke again. "I was dying to kiss her." "Why didn't you?"

"Didn't dare."

"Did you want to kiss her pussy?"

She wriggled, and under the toga I could see her legs come together as the thighs squeezed each other.

Then, boldly she answered, "Yes."

"And did you want her to kiss your pussy."

This time the "Yes" was a whisper.

I moved up close to her and bent my head to her. "Kiss me. I've just been kissing her pussy. You can taste it on my lips. Lick them with your tongue."

It was a dry lips kiss, but her tongue came out to lick me, and I turned it into a French kiss. She struggled at first then relaxed. I released her, took her hand and placed it on my prick.

" That little fellow has been inside her pussy. She liked to kiss it, you can taste her on it too." She thought about it and then bent down to give the kiss of life to my cock. Its response took her by surprise as it filled her mouth. She snatched it out, then began rubbing it against her cheek. Humphrey had made another convert.

"Would you like me to kiss your pussy, or is your friend going to?" I asked.

She made no reply, continuing to focus her attention on Humphrey, but I saw her legs squeeze together. It was response enough. I moved so she was underneath me and pulled the bottom of her toga up past her calves and knees, pausing as it reached her thighs. Her legs were shapely, but they were held close together. I inserted a finger gently between them, but they would not part. I continued lifting the toga until it revealed a pair of regulation black gym knickers. I started rolling them down, waiting for some reaction beneath me, but she was still occupied. As her bush came into sight I bent and put my mouth to it, licking with my tongue as I continued rolling the knickers down. Her thighs relaxed and I slipped my hands between them. She was more than ready. I wasted no time in dragging the garment down, her knees bending to allow access as her legs opened and my tongue was inside. She was a natural for 69, her clit begged for attention and it was obvious mine weren't the first lips to explore it, though they could have been the first male ones.

Then another pair of hands rolled me away, so that I lay on my back. Her friend had decided to join the action. I didn't have to bother undressing her, she'd already disrobed revealing a pair of boobs that would bring instant erections. She took her friends hands off my prick and replaced them with her own.

"I thought you preferred pussy", I said.

"Not always. I used to practice with my brothers, but yours is the biggest I've ever seen."

She began giving me the best fellatio I'd ever had. Though Humphrey had been occupied all evening, she took it into realms he had never experienced before.

She paused to murmur : "Do you want to come?"

"Not yet. I want to know how you learned to do this. If you could teach that you'd make a fortune."

She laughed and continued toying with it.

"I told you, I used to practice on my brothers. I was about 12 and they used to have competitions to see who could shoot the furthest. I was the judge. Tim, he's the eldest always won. So I said to Leslie that I would work him next time, to see if it made any difference."

"You wanked him?"

"Yes. But Lesley forgot all about the competition, and I did too. I played with it, and felt him coming and then brought him off with my mouth. He made a lot of noise and I thought someone would hear us but we had our record player on. Then of course Tim was upset, so I did him too. They didn't bother with competitions any more.

"Of course they had to tell their friends about their new game and they all wanted to try it. They used to bring their sisters round to see how it was done, and then of course we started swapping. It was more fun doing it with someone else's brother. Then of course we learned how nice it was to have a boy doing it to you.

"Do you want to come now?"

"Yes."

I reached out to her friend, and pulled her towards me so that she could sit on my face. I didn't give her the very best attention, the concerto being played on my cock, took all my concentration until it reached its finale. My back arched as I thrust up in one big come which the organist took in her mouth. As I subsided, she drained every last drop from it.

"That's three I know you've had" she said, stroking it. "That is a very powerful penis. By the way, I'm Anita, this is Diana… I heard you referred to as Tony."

I took the proffered hands and we all muttered the obligatory "How do you do's" rather incongruously.

"We can now talk if we meet again" said Anita, still stroking my prick while Diana's pussy was still resting against my face."

"Did you really fancy Ingrid, and want to kiss her pussy?" I asked.

It was Diana who answered. "Well, yes and no. I'm glad now I didn't, but she is a fascinating woman, you obviously thought so" she added challengingly.

"I'd just split up with my boyfriend, he was a real shit, Anita was having trouble with her's, and seeing all these girls idolising Miss Cartwright I thought there might be something in having a big strong woman like her as a companion."

"But she's not a dyke" I said.

"I know now" Anita agreed, "Not after the way you were rogering her. She was loving every minute of it. Seeing you going at it knocked every idea of lesbianism out of my head."

She bent over to kiss Humphrey and stroke it into life. "If I pump it up, have you got time to give me a few strokes", "Me too" Diana added.

If anyone could have aroused it, it would have been Anita, but she could only get it up into a rubbery replica which fell as she tried to sit on it. The best I could do was use my fingers to play with her.

My diary was getting more and more filled, Humphrey had more than enough on his plate. Tomorrow the Double Dees which would probably mean the weekend, which also involved an energetic rugby match, Ingrid on Wednesday and I still had to make my peace with Helen, which reminded me, had she seen my current company? I looked around, but could see nothing of her and the Butcher. Tuesday was still vacant, but I thought I had better pencil that in for Helen, and I'd probably need a rest on

Thursday after Ingrid. "Where do you get to on Fridays?" I asked.

"We usually have a little dinner party at my house" said Anita. "My parents spend the weekend on their gin palace. Would you like to have dinner with us?"

"I'd enjoy it very much. I'll save my strength for it."

"Do" said Anita. "We all want to have a satisfying evening."

I smiled, and moved my fingers in and out of her pussy.

"That's not quite the same" she said. "Nor is that" she added, as I bent down to kiss it. "But it is nice."

"Come on" said Diana, who had missed out on attention. "Everyone's going."

The place was emptying. "Let's go."

We stood up, and gathered our scanty garments. I didn't bother to take Diana's knickers, I couldn't claim them as a win. Friday perhaps, though I hoped she'd wear fancier ones, if any. "What time and where?" I asked.

"I've got nothing to write on" answered Anita. "I'll see you at the match, might even give your back a scrub."

The prospect was horrendous. Helen, the Double Dees and now these two. I might have to go sick.

Chapter Seven : Gran's Audition

As soon as she picked up the letter, Mother's face reflected gloom. "It's from MY mother." The emphasis was clear. "Probably to tell me she's going to get married again." Her faced lightened as she read the contents. "No, it's not as bad as that, she wants me to go over next weekend, Mother's Day. Doesn't mention you though. I'll have to give her a ring and remind her that's she's a Granny."

Grandmother hated to be reminded of the fact. Whether she actually forgot me, or pretended to, was a mystery. She timed her visits to London to coincide with school term so she didn't have to be reminded of our relationship. She refused to grow old, claimed age was a state of mind, and banished it from her thoughts. Since grandfather died, all I knew about her was what appeared in the glossy magazines. Like Mother, she spent her time on charitable activities, which also meant a great deal of socialising with people of like minds, and the glossies had constant photographs of her at some function or other. Even allowing for the quality of the paper, she looked pretty good. Mother said she'd had some nips and tucks done.

It was with reluctance that Grandmother extended the invitation to me, and then only on condition that I called her 'mother', definitely not 'grandmother'. She had, she told Mother, also invited some other friends. Whilst they would be able to understand her having a teenage son, a teenage grandson could ruin her position in society. Mother's relationship had never, ever, been explained. She had long called her mother by her first name, Nancy, and they were thought to be sisters, or cousins or childhood friends. It was never explained and no-one bothered to ask.

It was easy to think of them as sisters, I realised, when I saw them together for the first time in many years. Mother had driven us down in her E-Type. It was usually left with a nearby car showroom, who used it for a window attraction, and in return kept it in perfect condition. Mother always used black cabs in town, had an account with a company who usually managed to find a cab for her within minutes of her phoning for one.

"You get an awful lot of taxi rides for the price of just one tow-away" she answered when I asked why she didn't use the car more often. "It's not only a lot safer for a girl, but there's no risk of the car being vandalised."

Hood down, scarf round her hair she made an eye-catching sight through the villages as we drove down to Grandmothers'. We got the eyeful however, as we parked the car in front of the house and walked round to the grounds. It was like taking a trip through space and finding oneself on a beach on a Greek island. It was a normal weekend country-house party, some people playing croquet, others taking the sun, men in Panama hats, talking with girls in Hermes scarves.

What made it so different however was that from the neck down everyone was naked.

One woman broke away from a group to greet us. "Darling. How you've grown" she said, advancing on me, her breasts bouncing, and giving me a maternal hug with the customary peck on each cheek. She bestowed her attention on Mother, "Darling, thank you for bringing Tony down."

Mother was furious. "Why is everyone naked? What are you up to? If you'd let me know we wouldn't have come."

"Didn't I tell you? I thought you knew. I've taken up naturism. Met these people when I was in Turkey, they hardly ever wear clothes, so much better for you, and" she bent to whisper in Mother's ear, "so much cheaper too. Remember how much you had to spend on clothes just to go away for the weekend, doesn't cost a thing now. Off you go, get your clothes off and join us. Shoo, shoo." She waved us away, imperiously.

Well, if Mother was right and grandmother had been to a plastic surgeon for some nips and tucks, she'd got value for money. Posing as sisters wasn't an impossibility. She was more mature than Mother, but not that much so. There was no cellulite on her thighs, and while she'd never pass the pencil test to work as a showgirl, her D-cup breasts, bigger than Mother's, had nipples that stuck out rather than down. As she turned to rejoin her friends I could see that her bum didn't have the smooth shape of Mother's, there were creases in it. No doubt they would be ironed out in due course.

"She didn't mention it was going to be a nudist party because she knew I'd have refused to come. She might like to parade in the altogether, trying to hook a man, but I don't, and I don't think it's a good idea for you" she said. "How do you feel about it? We could just jump into the car and drive. On the other hand, as we're out in the country we might as well enjoy it. Stay in a hotel somewhere?"

"Oh, I'm game if you are" I replied. "Only your mother is going to lose a lot of HER admirers once you take YOUR clothes off. Not sure I like the idea of a lot of old men ogling you, and nobody's wearing anything, not even a thong.

"It makes for a very interesting situation" I added. I'm supposed to be Nancy's son, and therefore your nephew, or cousin or even boyfriend, depending upon whatever relationship people think you and your mother have. So, while I can be familiar with you and keep the others off, I can't be too friendly in case Nancy gets suspicious. It is going to be an interesting weekend."

It was, particularly when we found we had been given adjoining rooms, and there was a door between. There was a door on the other side of my room, leading, as I learned later, to grandmother's room.

Undressing didn't take long. The delay came because Mother found a bottle of Champagne in an ice bucket in her room, with two glasses. "Wonder whom she thought I'd share this with" Mother mused as she opened it. "Doubt if she thought it would be with you."

I sat on the edge of her bed and admired her yet again. The sun streaming through the window was like a spotlight on her, emphasizing the fairness of her hair which shone in the light. As she filled her own glass, I reached out to stroke her pussy. It was already moist, it always was, we jokingly referred to ourselves as the 'Ever-readies'. She retaliated by gripping my organ which immediately sprang to attention. We laughed at the immediate response as she manoeuvred herself to impale it. She eased herself up and down a few times so that her juices flowed. It was a comfortable way to drink champagne, she facing me, giving the occasional stroke up and down, me squeezing her nipples, hard enough to cause a little gasp of excitement.

With a couple of glasses of champagne each inside us, we were prepared to face the audience on the lawn. It was as I expected, the hubbub of conversation broke off as we reached the grass, and began the walk to join the group. Everyone turned to stare. I was attempting to be bold, and I knew Mother was tense although neither of us showed it. All eyes were on Mother, her pert breasts still faintly sun-tanned, her pussy still with the tide mark that showed she didn't sunbathe completely nude - though she would do in future.

Gran a.k.a. Nancy came a few yards to greet us and threw an arm out in a general introduction, "Everyone, this is Jane and Tony." There was a chorus of response to which she added to us, "You'll get to know their names during the weekend. You've timed it right, they're setting up the buffet already. Jane" she commanded "get some champagne and some glasses, they're over there, while I have a chat with my 'son '". She gave me a steady look as she emphasized the word. As Mother walked off, the eyes turned to watch her movement, the long slim legs, the jigging of her unrestrained breasts. Several cameras suddenly appeared, were trained on her and fired. I didn't doubt that they would appear in some publication.

"Let's have a look at you" said Nancy. She took me by the shoulders and turned me round. "Go on, turn" she said, standing back. "Let me see what my daughter has reared."

Obediently I spun, forgetting my half-hard which pirouetted in front of me.

"Good shoulders, good waist, Rugby I gather" she said approvingly. She felt my biceps and ordered, "Tense them." I did as she asked, and she put both hands around my upper arm, squeezing it as hard as she could. It was a sensual act which she followed up by standing back to inspect my thighs. My cock was still in the half-hard state of one deprived of an orgasm. Her eyes were on it as she added, "Strong legs too, and this," cupping it in her hand and squeezing it, "looks as if it will give a good account of itself when the time comes." I knew then that she intended to be there when that time came.

Mother rejoined us with glasses and a bottle. While she was filling the glasses Nancy said, "Fine boy, but we'll have to keep an eye on him. There are some men here who'll want to take him in hand." She made no mention of women.

It was as expected. Wherever Mother went in the group, the men followed. I had already been discounted as a possible rival - much too young - though my between-the-legs equipment caused a few speculative eyes to gaze on it. Nancy had her own followers, ever anxious to fill her glass, or offer a plate of canapes. Mother too had no shortage of disciples anxious that no want should be unfulfilled. My glass was never empty either. Somehow, I'd found a bunch of middle-aged admirers.

We'd learned all about choirmasters and gym teachers as ten year olds. Scoutmasters and choir masters were the danger for boys, even after their teens, while girls had to beware guide captains and gym mistresses. Only when we almost reached maturity did we find ourselves prey to the bishops, in the case of boys and girls. Religion was a jungle.

I was a hunter, not a victim. I couldn't cope with the lust in these men's eyes. Mother had been keeping

a close eye on me. I caught her glance and the raised eyebrows of the question. My response was an immediate nod towards the house. Her agreement was just as quick.

I murmured some excuse about toilet, ignoring the comment about watering the hedge, and sauntered back to the house. Somehow, Mother had beaten me to it and was already in her room. She was seething. "I've had a lot of dirty old men leching over me, and you've had another lot of dirty old men leching over you. Whatever can my mother think she's up to?"

I couldn't think of an answer.

"We've got this dinner party this evening. We'll go through that and we'll leave first thing tomorrow. O.K.?"

It was more than O.K. Now I knew what girls like Mother felt every day of their lives. If you were physically attractive you hid it in public, loose sweaters, dirty jeans. Only on private occasions did they, like a chrysalis, blossom into a butterfly.

She opened the adjoining door to my room and held it open. "I'm going to bed – to sleep" she added with a grin. "In the words of your schoolmates, I'm screwed, knackered, fucked. I've got to have some sleep. So just in case you go out, and some busybody comes into your room, I'm going to lock both doors. See you later sweetheart." A quick kiss, a longer one could have had a different reaction, and the door was shut behind me. I heard the key turn in the lock.

I wasn't at all sleepy. From my window I could see the changing formation of the guests down below. The patterns had formalised. The gay guys had given up the idea of fresh meat - me - for the moment, and were now rearranging positions. The gay girls would have killed rather than sacrifice their partners, and were now side by side, which left only the heteros, uncertain, as ever, who to make a play for.

Nancy wasn't among them. She had, I surmised, already made for her target. She had, but who the target was I learned a few minutes later, when there was a knock on the communicating door between her room and mine.

The lock was on her side, and she had turned the key, for the door opened as soon as I turned the handle. Nancy, my grandmother was on the other side on her hands and knees.

"I'm so glad you're here Tony. I'm in desperate straits. You can help me. Come on."

She fell to pawing the carpet in her bedroom. For a change, Nancy was dressed. If you counted a mauve bra and matching panties as clothes. The panties covered her essential, but the bra didn't help the two globes which were responding to the pull of gravity and brushing the carpet into a corner.

"I've dropped an earring" she explained, "it's a diamond one, rather valuable. It's in the carpet somewhere."

It was a shag-pile carpet, finding an earring in it wasn't going to be easy.

"Let's get organised" I said.

"You kneel there, side by side with me so that when you brush your hands across the carpet they just meet mine doing the same thing. Got it?"

The room was filled with her scent. The upper layer was her perfumes that crept out of her wrists, arms and neck. But at carpet level it was a more primitive odour. I had smelled it as soon as the door was opened. The musk given off by a woman in heat.

It was a mad, unbelievable situation. There was I, stark naked, kneeling, my penis touching the floor next to my grandmother, who had only the tiniest panties and whose breasts also greeted the carpet. I was seized with a fit of laughter and collapsed full length on the carpet. Tears came to my eyes.

"It's so funny" I said between bursts of laughter.

"If anyone came into this room now, what on earth would they think we were doing."

I tried to wipe the tears away with my hand, and then spotted a box of paper hankies by her bed. As I reached across for it, my penis touched something cold.

It brought on another bout of laughter. "Now what's so funny?"

"I think I've found your earring." "Where?"

"You'll never guess."

I turned so I was lying on my side. "Give me your hand." I took it and slipped it, palm down, under my penis.

She withdrew her hand and in the palm was a diamond earring. She put it in her ear immediately. "Clever dick. Clever, clever dick." she chanted, "It deserves a reward. What reward would a clever dick like this want?" she asked, looking across at me provocatively. "It certainly deserves a thank-you kiss."

She bent down to it and gave it a brief kiss on the tip, looking up at me coyly. Then she lifted it in her hand and ran her tongue around the tip. The response was immediate. In a fraction of a second the blood had surged in, stiffening it into its twelve full inches that needed both her hands to control as it reared against her face. She squealed in delight, and her mouth opened to take in its tip. I reached behind her and undid her bra strap, letting her breasts drop into my hands. I teased the nipples while she did her best to engulf my cock. I rolled her onto her back and straddled her and drove it into her throat so that she almost choked. But she pulled it out and began massaging herself with it, her eyes, her cheeks, her ears and then down to her breasts, massaging it between her nipples. I let her play with it while I lifted her buttocks up and began peeling off her purple panties. She lifted up her knees to make my task easier. Once I had them in my hand I wiped her mound of Venus with them, and put them to one side, a new addition to my pillow collection.

The scent of her pussy was overwhelming. I thrust my mouth onto it. Even with her mouth full she managed a scream of delight as I slurped into her pussy. It was a real mound that protruded between her thighs with a clitoris that could be held easily between thumb and finger, or teeth. My teeth nibbled it while she squirmed beneath me, gloating as she rolled my cock all over herself.

It was time for Humphrey to be fed. Mother had Christened it Humphrey after a dog in her village. Apparently it could smell a bitch on heat for miles around and would go to inordinate lengths to service her. Until now, her Humphrey was of a singular nature, but things were about to change, though they were still being kept in the family.

Like her daughter, Nancy was unassuming when it came to sex. She was prepared for anything, and would do anything. She knew immediately what to do as I changed my position on top of her. Without letting go of Humphrey she guided it into her pussy and arched her back so that she took every bit of it inside her. She sighed with pleasure as I thrust and her lips parted into a silent whistle. Slowly, I began moving inside her while she at first started murmuring "Yes, yes, that's it, that's it," which got louder and louder until she was shouting as her body quivered in one giant orgasm.

She shook and shuddered for what seemed an age, deep-throating me with her kisses, putting my hands on her breasts whenever I stopped paying attention to them. At last, she subsided, and moved from underneath me. We were both dripping sweat. I rolled onto my back alongside her. Frustrated again, Humphrey was once more half-hard, and lay on my thigh, pointing towards her. She reached out to it and raised it up, before leaning over to give it a salute with her lips and tongue.

"He's a beautiful feller. He's given me more than I've ever had in my life. Now I know what sex is all about. A bit late to discover it, but just in time. Humphrey and I will be seeing a bit more of each other, but in the meantime, now I've got my earrings, I'd better get dressed for dinner. What did I do with those purple pieces?"

I saw the bra, collected it and gave it to her, the panties were concealed in my hand. I showed them to her. "They're mine, they'll be under my pillow, but first", I used them once again to dry her pussy. Twirling them in my hand, I opened the door and returned to my own room. I used one of the plastic bags in the bathroom to wrap them in and buried them in the bottom of my case. The plastic bag would help contain the perfume of her pussy.

Chapter Eight : The Sculptress

Nancy was my first visitor once I was back at school. I was invited for tea and crumpets at her hotel in the town, the invitation card read, a taxi would be sent to collect me. Matron gave me the card, and I wondered if she saw the significance of the wording of the invitation. Though the Double Dees were part of the school's establishment, not to mention Anita, who practised fellatio on her brothers, and her friend Diana, the first week back at school gave no time for social studies. Afternoon tea and crumpet would be perfect. How perfect I was to find out.

Nancy was waiting to meet me at reception. She looked as if she was about to be photographed for a Vogue cover.

"You look gorgeous" I said. She gave me a chaste kiss on the cheek, took my arm and led me to the lift. "I think you've grown, and you look very handsome" she said. She'd taken a suite, and to my surprise, the table was laid for tea. I'd only expected crumpet. She lifted the cover off a dish. Buttered crumpets. Then I saw there were three places set.

"I've invited a friend for tea as well. It's all part of a big surprise for you." There was a tap on the door. Nancy opened it and ushered in her friend, a woman in her late twenties, not afraid to wear short skirts, very self-possessed and quite attractive. She carried a large holdall.

"Perfect timing said Nancy. "Joyce, I'd like you to meet Tony. Tony this is Joyce, she's a sort of sculptor.

She's going to do a sculpture of you. Now, let's have tea. Tony, pass the crumpet around."

I noticed that both women smiled at the remark. The conversation was kept to school. I told them as much as I thought they ought to know. What sort of sculpture I wanted to know? Later, they answered.

"Anyone like any more?" asked Nancy as the teapot was empty. Neither of us did. "Right. Let's adjourn." She led the way to the bedroom. So it was going to be a threesome I thought. I wasn't quite so certain when Joyce took command. She'd brought her holdall with her and set it down at the foot of the bed.

"Right" she said, advancing on me. Let's see what we've got to work on. Stand still Tony."

Nancy stood to one side and watched. Joyce took off my blazer, then my tie. She kicked off her shoes and dropped to her knees in front of me. I could look down her blouse. She wore half-cup bras, which supported from below, but I could see the tops of her breasts, even the nipples. They were a pair to be proud of, and as she undid the belt on my trousers, then unzipped the fly I wondered if I was going to have a chance to undress her.

My trousers were at my ankles and wouldn't come off without taking my shoes off. She bent down to undo the laces. The skirt was taut on her buttocks, and I noted that there was no visible panty line, v.p.l. which meant she either wore tights or didn't wear panties. Off came my shoes, I lifted first one foot then the other so that the trousers could be taken off. I thought she wasn't going to bother about my socks, but they came off too.

"Men look very undignified when they're wearing nothing but their socks" she said, handing them to Nancy. The same advice had been given to me by my very first lover. I always followed it. Socks came off before my trousers.

"But why is it that a woman with nothing on but stockings looks at her sexiest?" I countered.

"Ah" said Nancy, "that's a woman's secret." She smiled, and I smiled back. It was a pose I had seen her in more than once.

Joyce was busy undoing the buttons on my shirt, and slipping it over my arms. It left only my boxer shorts. The whole scene had been so clinical, Nancy watching the undressing, gathering my clothes in her arms as they were handed to her like a nurse in a hospital ward, that I was a long way from getting an erection. The occasional glimpse of her nipples was the only excitement for me as Joyce slid my underpants down my thighs and calves. I lifted one foot then the other, a limp Humphrey almost brushing her nose as I did so.

"I'm not surprised he's bashful" she said holding everything in her hands and weighing them. "But even in this state he's quite heavy. I wonder if he can punch his weight."

Nancy could have answered but chose not to, an enigmatic smile crossing her lips.

Joyce turned to Nancy. "This is where I start work, and I like to work in private. Do you mind? Give me a couple of hours. There are a lot of preliminaries to be done."

She escorted Nancy to the bedroom door and locked it behind her. She came back to me. "Any idea what this is about?" she asked, and began undoing her blouse. I shook my head.

She took her blouse off and turned her back to me. "You can give me a hand, I gave you one."

I undid her bra, and threw it to a chair. She turned round. She didn't need a bra, her breasts were beautifully firm. I cupped them in my hands, and squeezed the nipples.

"Why do you wear a bra? These don't need them." I jiggled them in my hands, squeezed the nipples and bent to bite them. She winced, but made no move to stop me.

"When you were taking my trousers off I could look down and see them: They're wonderful."

I continued holding them as she undid her skirt, letting it drop to the floor and stepping out of it.

"That's just why I wear that particular bra, so that my clients CAN look down my cleavage. Like you they don't know what's going to happen to them. It's always a surprise fixed up by a wife or girlfriend. When they see my breasts, they feel more comfortable, more excited. Men like to see breasts in a bra, its more sexy, and it gets them excited. That's how I want them to be so that when I ask them to take it off, they can't get to hold them quick enough, and look what happens then." She looked down.

I could feel things happening down below and so could she as Humphrey nudged the gap between her stockings and her fanny.

"Good boy" she said and reached down to grip it. "Wow. This is something worth casting. What I'm here for is to make a replica of this for your friend, so that when you're not with her, she can pretend that you are."

I got it then. Nancy wanted a dildo. "Will there be batteries in it?"

"In one, but we'll cast the other in stainless steel. That'll be a desk ornament, an executive toy." She undid her suspender belt, and sat on the bed.

"Help me get these stockings off."

I rolled one down, she the other. "Don't you ever wear panties?" I asked.

"Sometimes. I always have a pair with me, just in case, but I make them so wet, its uncomfortable. Why do you ask, do you like them?"

"I save them" I replied.

"Ah, I see. I must give you my pair before I go, or do you want them now?"

"Now."

She went to her jacket, and produced a pair from one of the pockets, green silk ones. "I'll put the cost on your friend's bill" she said, wiping them under my nose before putting them in my hand. I could smell her on them. She'd taken them off when they got wet. So my grandmother was now not even my mother, just a friend.

I bent down, and lifted her feet one by one to put her panties on. Then I slid them up her legs until they were where they should be. She was right, they were sopping wet in seconds. I held them in place for a minute, then peeled them off. For a 'thank you' I pressed my mouth against her fanny. Her clitoris came out like a mini-penis as my lips found it.

Joyce pushed me away. She was breathing heavily, but she shook herself. "Work first. We'll have some of that in a minute."

As she undid her holdall, producing an array of equipment, tubes, sprays, masks, a pair of scales, even a tape measure. I seized the chance to put her knickers in my shorts pocket. I hadn't won them yet, but I was sure that I would.

She picked up the tape measure, "You can guess what this is for" she said. "Stand up." She dropped to her knees and held Humphrey down in a horizontal position. "Think dirty thoughts" she said. "Think of what you'd like to do to my breasts and my pussy."

I felt Humphrey grow as I obeyed. She squeezed it gently, gave the foreskin a couple of strokes and then measured his length. "Twelve and three quarter inches" she said in an awed voice. She wrote the figures down on a pad. "Bloody Hell. No wonder your friend wants to get it cast. It'll make a fortune as a dildo."

"Now the scales." She held them so that my cock and bails were in the container. "Two pounds and an ounce." She called the figure out again as if she couldn't believe it,

"Two pounds and an ounce, thirty three ounces. She stroked it and kissed it. "This fellow is the equivalent of four half-pound beefburgers. That's what they call a real beef dagger."

She stood up and put her arms around me, pulling me in tight. Her nipples were hard, and Humphrey was brushing against her stomach. She stood tip-toe so that he was between her legs, her moist pussy resting on it.

"Now we must be quick." She inserted a plastic straw down Humphrey's hole, "Mustn't get any in there" she said, picked up one of the sprays and discharged a warm liquid over every bit of him. She left it for a second, then came the second which required much greater attention. Having sprayed from above, Joyce lay on her back, under Humphrey, directing the spray at every part of the cock and balls which loomed above her.

Satisfied, she stood up, her breasts bouncing again. Seeing my eyes on them she came over and lifted my hands to them. "Squeeze them as hard as you like. Keep thinking dirty thoughts, like how you're going to kiss my pussy, and how I'm going to kiss your prick. Because I am, as soon as the latex is cured. I can't wait to get my lips around it, and have it sink deep into my pussy. I'm not even sure that mine's big enough to take it, though I'm going to give it a good try. But for my sculpture, the bigger it grows the better. Do you have a name for it?"

"Humphrey" I admitted. Humphrey at that moment had swollen to its biggest ever size. But it felt like it was wearing a wet-suit. Joyce's 'talk dirty" technique worked. I half-bent over to give her nipples some attention from my mouth. She pressed my head hard against them.

"Humphrey. That's a nice name. I call mine Jessie."

"I didn't know girls gave theirs' names."

"I did. After all, she's my best friend."

"Would you like me to say hallo to her again?"

"She'd like that. She likes to meet people, especially boys. But don't let Humphrey touch anything. I don't think he's cured yet."

She put a tentative finger on him, then her hand. "He's done" she corrected. "Let me take this overcoat off him."

She sat me on the bed so that I was bracing myself against it. "You'll like this" she said and dropped to her knees.

She was right. It was a wonderful feeling as she unrolled the latex from my balls right down Humphrey's length. She held it out for me to see.

"It's just like a big condom."

"Yes, that's what it looks like. But just wait till you see the finished product." She put it in her holdall, brought out some cotton wool with liquid from a bottle and washed Humphrey thoroughly, stretching him so that she could get to every little crease.

"Now" she said, "let's call in some of those promises. "Didn't you want to say Hallo to Jessie."

She lay on the bed, her legs together, leaving me to tease them apart. I could tease too. I sat on her breasts, Humphrey resting on her stomach, touching her navel. Then I bent to kiss her pubes, my tongue pushing until it could first taste the inner lips of her fanny, then as her legs opened wider and wider, the labia and her clit.

I had my face buried in her pussy, holding her up by her buttocks, still holding her breasts down with my bottom, while she struggled beneath me, shouting a mixture a words not all of which were compliments. I sat up, turned round and squatted over her pussy.

"Bastard" she said. "I couldn't do a thing, couldn't even get hold of it. All I could do was bite your back." I hadn't felt it. "Not real bites" she added, "lip bites, more like kisses. What I wanted to do to Humphrey."

She was already making up for lost time. Her, hands were massaging Humphrey and she used him as an anchor so that she could slide down the bed until he was in her mouth. I waited for her to take it out, then pulled her up the bed until he was in position above her.

"I've never had one as big as this" she murmured. "Put it in gently, and don't come, not even if I do and I'm almost ready now. I want to do another sculpture when its wet with my juices."

We kissed, a long one, as Joyce fed Humphrey into her. The muscles in her vagina fastened on it, sucking it in. She stopped kissing me.

"That feels marvellous. I've got it all in." She began moving her bottom "That's it, that's it." We changed position several times, sometimes she on top, laughing as she rose in a crouch, almost on her feet to get to Humphrey's tip so that she impaled herself as she slid down his shaft. She was on all fours, and I was just entering her when she thrust me away. "Back to work."

The plastic straw went into the hole and there she was with her spray gun. I had to kneel as she covered every part of Humphrey with the spray.

"Do you know" said Joyce conversationally, lying on her back, her head resting on her folded arms.

Humphrey above her, his latex overcoat curing, "I don't think he's as big as last time. Screwing me has taken something off him."

She gave it a few more minutes, then peeled his overcoat off. She brought the cotton wool out and knelt down to wash him thoroughly. "You want it, don't you?" she said, looking up at me.

For answer, I bent down and lifted her onto the bed. She moved into a comfortable position, opened her legs and bent her knees so that I could see every part of her, from the outer lips, and as I parted them, the labia, the vulva and her joy, her clitoris. I climbed on.

I was just in time. Noises from the adjoining room indicated the return of Nancy. I gave Joyce one last thrust which brought a gasp from her, and climbed off.

I used her cotton wool to wash between her thighs and then my own. I dried her and then gave it a final kiss. "There'll be another time" she promised.

We dressed, made sure there were no obvious signs to indicate what we'd been doing. Joyce picked up her holdall, and unlocked the door.

Nancy rose from a chair. "Well?"

"Perfect" replied Joyce. "He was a very patient model. I think you'll be pleased with the results."

"When will that be?"

"About two weeks. I'll give you a call." From a pocket, she took some business cards. "That's my number, you might know someone else who would like me to sculpt them", she said with a significant look at me.

She shook my hand. "Thank you for your co-operation. You've been a wonderful model, you posed beautifully. Goodbye, and thank you both, for everything."

To Nancy she added, as they moved to the door. "It will look great on your desk. I'll see you at the club."

"Don't forget" said Nancy at the door, "One plastic and one stainless steel." So that was it. I was to be a penholder or something, just an executive toy.

As the door closed behind her, Nancy came over to give me a lustful kiss before leading me back to the bedroom. "I've got something to show you."

She stood in front of me, her arms stretched up, waiting for me to pull her dress up. It was just about the right height above the knee, and the straps just went over her shoulders, leaving them exposed. I pulled it over her head and as it came off, realised that she was wearing less clothes than ever. No bra, no panties just suspender belt and stockings.

"Now you" she said, undoing my trousers, leaving the shirt buttons to me. She pulled the trousers and shorts down together, not even bothering to take them off before grasping Humphrey and putting it to her mouth. "I've missed you" she said to him between kisses. "I've wanted you for weeks."

She stood in front of me, legs akimbo. "Well, notice anything?"

I wasn't sure what I was looking for. She sat down on the edge of the bed. Kiss my pussy" she demanded. I was about to do so when I saw it. The pain must have been intense as it was being done, and she winced as I touched first one, then the other, even gently, with a finger. A tattooist had been at work on each little plump piece of her buttocks that lay closest to her quim, the piece I always nipped with teeth.

On one, an angel was pointing with his bow to her pussy. On the other, a devil pointed his three pronged trident to her little bottom hole. The words "Heaven" for one and "Hell" the other were superfluous.

I didn't have much experience of bottoms. Since the school party when someone had tried to enter mine, I'd been a bit more adventurous, teasing them with my finger, sometimes sliding it in at just the right moment. But no more than that.

"Which am I going to enter?" I asked.

She held Humphrey. "I think it had better be Heaven."

"It was quite funny" she said. "I'd got the idea of the devil and the angel from a book. I found this tattooist in the Waterloo Road and told him what I had in mind. He was quite enthusiastic. He'd usually done L.O.V.E. and H,A.T.E. on soldiers' knuckles, and doing what I wanted was a challenge for him. What does it look like by the way, is it artistic? I've tried squatting over a mirror to see it, but I can't get the angle right."

"You can't tell at the moment" I said diplomatically. "It's still weeping a bit. Do you think I ought to put plasters on them?"

"No. He said it was best to let the air get to it. That's why I haven't got any panties on"

"Oh," I said, "I thought it was because you didn't want to waste any time."

"How did he do the tattoo, lie on the floor with his head and hands between your legs, or were you stretched out on the bed?"

"Not like that at all. He gave me a couple of local anaesthetics; spray first then a syringe, just like a dentist. Then he massaged that bit until I couldn't feel him massage, which meant it was frozen there. It was quite sexy, like having a doctor feel your breasts for cancer. You know its purely clinical and means nothing to him, though it gives you a thrill."

I didn't doubt that Mr Tattooist had got his thrills.

"I had to lie on my back on a big armchair, my legs over the back and spread as wide as possible. Like this."

She fell back on the bed and opened her legs. She was almost in the splits, and I knew then that she wouldn't feel any pain, as she obviously hadn't with the last man to penetrate her.

"Then what happened?"

"He started using the needle on me. He'd done two drawings of a devil and an angel which I loved. "Did you like them?" I nodded.

"He told me just to relax while he got on with his work. I think he gave me one while I was asleep because I was very wet when I woke up, and he didn't charge me. He said it had been a different experience, and if my friends wanted something similar he'd be happy to oblige."

"I bet he would" I said.

"If you sat on that chair, I could get on top without too much pain. Let's try it."

She bore it for a few minutes, but there was no pleasure for her or me, I didn't like to see her in pain. I lifted her off.

"Thank you for the tea and crumpets" I said. There had been two so it was plural. "I'll come again if you invite me."

She gave Humphrey a last squeeze and I nuzzled her breasts, biting her nipples in the way she liked. As I dressed she rang reception for a taxi. "Come to me for your next half-term. I'll find an excuse not to invite your mother."

I cupped her breasts and she held my balls through my trousers as she walked me to the door.

Chapter Nine : The Gymnast

Mother kept my mail. Only if the envelope was sufficiently important looking did she send it on to me at school. The only example was an OHMS envelop she sent on which contained an invitation to join the T.A. Other letters were left on my bed until I returned.

The brochure explaining the benefits to be derived from a newly opened aerobics gymnasium in Kensington almost passed me by. Something about the word aerobics caused me to take a second look at the photographs of the demonstrator.

Erika. No mistake. A gymnast in positions which, transferred to a bedroom would drive any man crazy. I knew then what she meant at the Double Dee party by promising me 'something special' later. She was offering me the chance of making 'later' into 'now.' And to emphasise the inducement, it offered special cheap rates to students prepared to act as demonstrators, or if good enough, paid instructors.

Mother and I had reached a plateau. Without spelling it out, we acknowledged that there was no future in our own relationship, and that we must each look elsewhere, but with the comfort of knowing that we didn't have to go far to find wonderful sex. If I came home and found her in bed I usually slipped in beside her and vice versa.

The faithful tracksuit and trainers were all I wore on half-term, it only required me to pick up the sports bag that contained everything I would need for any sporting activity, from a rugby match to a pool contest.

I bought a temporary membership ticket at the entrance to the gymnasium and volunteered my services as a demonstrator. The mail drop had brought a response. The gym was crowded. At the end, I could see Erika moving from group to group of her students. The gymnasium, still had its wall bars, its horses, boxes and in the corner, the weights.

I changed quickly, hung myself from the wall bars and began doing my abdominal exercise, raising my legs to the midway position, then lowering them. Several of the older men, recognised the exercise from their National Service days and joined in, collapsing when they realised they could barely lift their legs away from the bars, never mind match me in holding them straight out.

I saw Erika's eyes flicker to the little bit of action I had caused and knew she had registered me. I dropped off the bars and wandered across to where the bench press was still in position. The bar alone was 25 kilos I noticed, as I crawled under it,

"Hallo Tony" said her voice. She was undoing the clips at the end of the bars, and putting additional weights on. She lacked them in position and stood back,

"Now that is roughly my weight, seven and a half stone. Let's see how many times you can push me up and down. If you make ten, I'll show you the trick I promised you at the Double Dee party. "

Whether they knew the wager or not, I didn't know, but I was now surrounded. Perhaps I hadn't been unobtrusive in trying first the wall bars, then the weights -

no aerobics student would go near either. But they were all round me now, dying for me to fail at lifting her weight.

The first one, two, three, four, five even anywhere six are always easy. At seven you have to pause to consolidate your strength, ration it far what is to come. Eight is not too much of an effort, but you are then wondering how you got involved in this crazy contest. Erika knew a lot about strength, body-weight and muscle. Why else would she have picked on ten as my maximum figure?

I made nine, barely, and collapsed, my hands off the bar. The crowd was now divided between those who wanted me to succeed, and had begun to cheer me an, faltering now as I looked ready to collapse, and those who still wanted me to fail.

Then I felt someone straddle my legs, holding them down for me to lift against. I felt the warmth from that pussy surging through my calves. I gripped the bar, placed my hands in position and pushed up.

Ten.

I made sure to lock it in position at that point, didn't want it pinning me to the bench, and I didn't think I had the strength to lower it. I felt my legs being pulled out from the bench seat and I was hauled to my feet.

"Well done" said Erika, pressing a chaste kiss on my cheek. "You've got a job as a demonstrator, if you still want it. But shall we talk about it later?"

A few loosening up exercises and I was ready for anything, but a class hadn't been arranged for me and though there were many youngsters of my age, wanting to join me it would have to be next time.

They were the type of pupils any teacher of any subject would like to have. Clean eyed, straight limbed young men, girls just recently into maturity, high breasted, slim waists, with buttocks so firm a postcard could not be slipped between them. I made a mental note of those whose eyes strayed to the bulge in my shorts, and as they went to their dressing room explained that I was hoping to enrol a class next week, if they wanted to join....

I kept out of the way as the last instructor left, emerging only to join Erika as she began the ritual of lights off, burglar alarm on.

"Tread where I tread," she said. "Keep out of the beams."

I wasn't the only guest at this party. Her flat was filled with the instructors and demonstrators, all young and all very nubile.

Erika was being devilish. She waved her arm to where everyone was enjoying the wine and canapes.

"Tony" she called, and gestured to me, "has been a good friend of mine for", she emphasised the word 'good', "well, at least three months.

"He also has the unique, so far, distinction of being the only person to screw me in a swimming pool. At that time, I said I would show him something special as a counter. With your permission, I will do just that."

She wore only a tee shirt and shorts. In seconds they were discarded which caused a reaction among the other pupils who all stripped themselves. Erika stalked, there was no other word for it, across to me. She knew why I had hesitated at stripping, but she was obviously going to get her own back far neglecting her at the Double Dee party.

She used my tee shirt to pull me to my feet, pulling it off at the same time and throwing it aside. Then she dropped to her knees, undid my shorts and peeled them off. Humphrey was still limp, but the comparison between him and the pricks that dangled from the loins of the other boys was obvious.

Erika grasped it and used it to pull me into the centre of the room and told me to lie down. She called two of the other girls over to put some life into Humphrey. Their fondling and kissing had an immediate effect, and which brought him a crowd of admirers anxious to relieve the initial handmaidens.

Erika ushered them aside and stood astride me, her pussy directly above where Humphrey's shaft would be, but with her back to me. Then, just as I was thinking she was going to drop down and impale herself, she started to bend back. She was above me in an upside down position and gave my lips a kiss as she passed them, then my chest. Humphrey was lying on my stomach, his tip at my navel. She picked him up, kissed my navel and continued bending until her head was between her legs and Humphrey was pointing straight up at her. It was the same trick she performed at the double D's party, but this time she licked his tip then engulfed him and to applause from everyone, began to give him a blowjob.

It wasn't the end of her performance. She put her hands down on the floor and balanced herself on them while her legs came up into a perpendicular position, my cock deep inside her mouth. I hoped she didn't slip. If she did, there were only two alternatives, Humphrey would inspect her kidneys, or he would be bitten off in his prime.

There were couples already trying to emulate her feat as she took me on a tour of her flat. It was a very feminine bedroom and the bed was very comfortable.

"What did you think of my surprise?" she asked, preparing to continue with the blowjob while I renewed acquaintance with her labia and vulva."

"Wonderful, but like the last time you did it, I couldn't help thinking of the penalty if your hands slipped."

"Thought that might occur to you, but I've been a gymnast since infants school, never collapsed yet." "It certainly brings a variation to the back-bend but there's another improvement you could make" I added.

"Oh. What?"

"Just get another boy standing astride me but facing you. As you bend back, he gets a lovely view of your pussy and is in exactly the right position to drive straight into it."

"I'll give it a try later on, but first eat me properly and then fuck me hard."

Chapter Ten : The Pregnant Lady

I'd seen nothing of Ingrid at school. She had rung me and given me her address after the school leaving party as she'd promised, but we hadn't made lunch. I'd been somewhat preoccupied with one thing and another, and she had gone off for her holiday in France. It was Diana who gave me the news at the disco. Ingrid had met some rich Frenchman on holiday, and had married him. More, she'd learned a happy event was expected.

I gulped, and Diana gave me a half smile. She'd seen me rogering her at the party, and knew the earth had moved for us. "Had any other good news lately?" she asked sweetly.

As so often happens, no sooner does someone come into your thoughts than they become reality. Two days later I received an invitation to a party. Ingrid was saying farewell to the school and Britain, with an informal party at her flat, the theme being 'Finders keepers'.

A note added that two or three 'informal' ladies would also be welcomed. There was no mention of her marriage or pregnancy, so I rang her. She confirmed both and added in the formal tones of one whose conversation was being overheard, that she and her husband were very happy, that he was delighted at becoming a father and was looking forward to meeting her old, and new, friends at the party. The 'Finders Keepers' theme would be explained then.

In was obviously one for the Double Dees and Erika, she and Ingrid could exchange P.E. gossip, while Erika's party trick would be a riot.

Once again George and the Jaguar came to our aid. I crossed my fingers in the 'Fanites' position as I climbed into the back with the Double Dees, and George set off to pick up Erika.

"Spoilsport" said Daphne, taking my hand and slipping it down her blouse so I could caress her breasts. Dolores took the other hand and did the same. It's a very pleasant way to travel in any car.

Erika didn't even blink as she climbed in, taking the situation in at a glance. There was only one place left, so she undid my flies, pulled Humphrey out and began a very gentle blowjob. I hadn't been able to signal Fanites to her.

Ingrid's flat was one floor in a Victorian mansion block in St John's Wood, big, airy rooms with views looking across to Lords cricket ground. Although it was early afternoon, the curtains were drawn. Francis, her husband, was an international wheeler-dealer probably twenty years older than her, who spoke the slightly fractured English that Maurice Chevalier perfected.

Outside caterers had been brought in to provide the buffet and staff the bar. It was left to us whether we would partake or not. I gave Ingrid the customary kiss on both cheeks and shook the hand of her husband. Firm handshake, that was a plus. His greeting of my companions was a much more drawn out introduction. The twins were eye-catchers anywhere, both good-lookers who knew it, and dressed to tease, mini-skirts showing long legs and blouses loose enough for a hand to slip down, as I'd already discovered. They had taken the 'informal' part of the invitation seriously.

It was as if they and Erika had discussed outfits, for she was the exact counterpoint, skintight white Anitas that showed every crease of her body, and that she obviously wasn't wearing panties, and a white tee shirt, tight enough for her nipples to be seen. Her breasts weren't as big as those of the Double Dees but they were just as joyful. Francis gave them his best attention as he greeted them. I caught Ingrid's eye and she smiled.

"Nice friends you've got. Glad you haven't missed me too badly."

We joined the party. Ingrid's farewell to the school hadn't extended to inviting any of her former colleagues fortunately, we were just introduced as her friends to a mixed group of the French population of London, some contemporaries' of his, others much younger, and Ingrid's own chums, some from her days at PE college whom Erika also knew. Everyone had taken the informal aspect seriously, no-one was overdressed.

Relaxed attitude became even more relaxed as the party spirit prevailed. Few people noticed the tables being cleared and removed and the staff going with them. As the door closed behind them, the lights were lowered, and conversation ceased. Everyone waited.

"All got full glasses?" Ingrid called, walking to the centre of the room. Behind her, Francis was arranging chairs into four ranks of four. She waited until everyone made sure their glasses were filled. "Right. I give you a toast, 'To Britain and its people'. Bottoms up." Everyone drank.

"Now, I did say this was a Finders Keepers, informal party. It's been pretty informal so far, but its going to get even more informal from now on. If you count up, you'll see we're equal numbers, sixteen gentlemen, sixteen ladies, who will soon be sixteen men and sixteen women. In a few minutes the ladies will leave the room and take their tops off. The gentlemen will then take their trousers off and sit on one of the chairs. All the lights will go off and the ladies will come back in. What they find they keep. So if you have your eye on a particular target make sure you know the shape of her breasts and what material her skirt or trousers are made of in the case of the men, and for women, whether he's wearing a shirt or jumper or some sort of jewellery. They'll be the only clue you'll get.

To make things a little bit easier, we'll have a five minute touching session with the lights off. With that, the room was plunged into darkness.

As she was talking, I was surreptitiously moving to a position near the light switch. Having flicked it up and plunged the room into darkness, it took only two steps before she was alongside me and our arms were round each other.

"It's no good feeling this fabric, it'll be off" she said, giggling in my ear as I fondled her breasts. "So will these" I answered, as her hand gripped Humphrey through my trousers. We said nothing for several minutes, enjoying a long passionate kiss. I tried several times to break, there were so many questions I wanted to ask, but each time she whispered "Later" and went back to a kiss.

I heard a soft 'ting' from the watch on her wrist against my ear. "Another minute" she whispered. "Listen, take the chair furthest away in the back row, the one at the far end. I'll find you there."

"What about your husband?"

"He's OK. He's after one of your twins, but I think they've got their eyes on other people. Don't forget, furthest away, back row." She moved away from me.

"Right, split up now. Don't signal your intentions" she called out, and there was a general shuffling as people re-arranged positions so as not to give away their particular targets.

When the lights came on they revealed a rather dishevelled bunch of people. The careful hairdo's and make-up jobs had gone, but there were mischievous grins and lustful looks, bulges in trousers and out-thrust nipples.

"Come on ladies" Ingrid called out and opened the door. Blouses were already coming off as they filed outside and the door shut. I made for the chair at the far end of the back row right away. Francis I noticed had claimed that at the near end of the front row, as far from mine as possible, but nearest the light switch.

"Ready?" he called. It was a bizarre sight, rows of naked bottoms and legs - some still with socks - like an orgiastic school assembly. The light went out.

The door opened and there was a rush of air and a bustle of bodies. Ingrid took no chances, she was sitting on my lap, her skirt around her waist with a limp little Humphrey between us in seconds. A press-stud and a zip were undone and I took my hands off her naked breasts to pull the skirt over her head. I'd already taken my shirt off, she didn't need to know what fabric it was.

Around us were cries of astonishment and pleasure, "Come on" said Ingrid, climbing off me and taking my hand. It was her flat so she had an advantage, she had no trouble finding the bar in the darkness. Behind it someone had placed a number of cushions. We sank onto them.

"I'll have to be careful. I don't want to hurt it." I said.

"Don't be stupid. I'm only three months pregnant, nothing you're likely to do is going to hurt our son. Yes, it is yours." Now let me hold its cause, while you can attend to its effect."

We had taken up the positions automatically, our heads between each others' legs. I was kissing the cool insides of her thighs, my teeth nipping the little mound of flesh on each side of her quim, my right arm under her thigh so I could part its inner lips and get my tongue inside. It needed only a minor exploration before her clitoris came seeking my tongue, and the little electric shock sparked between us.

I felt my cock jerk and Ingrid's lips closed on it, her tongue coursing the rim at the join of the foreskin. I was missing the touch of her breasts, and slid a hand between us to feel a nipple. She answered by rolling on her back, giving me room to turn. We had a long, lingering kiss licking each other's juices with our mouths, my hands squeezing her nipples, her's holding Humphrey and guiding him between her thighs. Her legs gripped my waist as I pushed in,

"Perhaps you'd better not go in as far as you did last time, I'd forgotten how big he is, he's filling me right up." She nibbled my ear. "You know I still fantasise about you daring to screw a teacher, and then finding how big it was and how well you could use it."

"Not as much as I fantasised about holding these" I answered, bending to kiss the nipples of the two orbs I held in my hands. "They're beautiful, and to think they'll get bigger."

"And probably lose their shape so that no-one, not even you, will want to fondle and kiss them any more. And all because of this" giving my cock an extra squeeze with the muscles of her vagina.

"I bet this time next year they'll be just the same as they are now" I answered.

"Give it six months from the time he's born and you could be right. Do you want to talk or fuck?"

"Both." I rolled so we were again side by side, my hands on her breasts, my prick deep inside her, keeping up a gentle thrusting movement as we talked. "Did you want to marry Francis?"

"Oh Yes. He's fun, he's got plenty of money, he likes pretty women and he's dying to be a father. We've got a wonderful relationship. I don't want him to suspect the baby isn't his, or that I'm fucking you now, and may do again."

"But how.. when..?"

She cut me off. "We're keeping this flat on. Our base in this country, and obviously it would be nice if someone we knew could spare the time to keep an eye on it. I know it's a bit of a drag coming down from school every now and again to make sure the place hasn't been burgled or flooded, but Francis will make some financial arrangement. I'll be popping over every now and again to see my gynaecologist."

She gave me a deep kiss and began to move more quickly on me.

"I'll give you a key before you go, now fuck me."

If I needed any encouragement, the sighs, the gasps and the occasional suppressed orgasm around me would have been all I needed. I rolled her onto her back, squeezed the nipple of one breast, braced myself with the other and drove into her.

"Lovely, beautiful, no don't be careful, it's perfect, harder, harder" I bounced her thoroughly and as she came, her teeth bit into my shoulder, great shuddering gasps, muffled against my skin. "Now you." She altered her position slightly, and squeezed her cunt muscles so that my cock's tip was being massaged by a part of her pussy. I came immediately, a roar from the back of my throat which brought giggles from three ladies scattered about the room who recognised it.

We lay still, getting our breath back, my hands on her breasts, feeling her heart gradually quietening, her hand feeling my pulse through a limp Humphrey. I heard the faint ting of the alarm on her watch.

"Time to be discreet" she said, and pulled me to her for a last deep kiss and fondle. She crawled away and stood up, and I followed. There was movement all round. I joined someone at the bar who was pouring wine into a glass - not an easy thing.   I found my way back to my chair. I could sense that other chairs were occupied.

"Before I put the light on, to save embarrassment, it might be as well if the gentlemen resumed their seats. I don't think it matters about dressing though. Everyone ready?"

There was a murmured 'Yes' and the light came on, very low, followed by the distinctive sound of champagne bottles being opened.

"Champagne everyone" said Francis, a bottle in each hand as everyone rushed to find a glass. Ingrid was behind him with two more bottles, and some of the Frenchmen were opening others. At first it was surreptitious looks, but then they became more admiring as men admired breasts and legs, and girls were equally outspoken about the males.

The Double Dees equipment was admired and envied, while the more discerning men yearned to caress the long slim legs, and erect breasts of Erika.

Inevitably, it was Daphne who set the ball rolling. She came over, grasped me firmly by the balls and kissed me on the lips.

"A spent force now" she said, squeezing it and looking round to where everyone was gazing with amusement. "I was trying to get to it but someone beat me. I heard it fire, wonder who provided the receptacle?"

She looked challengingly all round to the other girls who giggled and shook their heads.

Not to be outdone, I cupped both breasts and kissed her. "I hope you're glad you came?"

She went over to a good-looking young Frenchman, and taking his cock in one hand, putting the other arm round his shoulder said "Thank you for having me."

If there had been any awkwardness about seeing each other naked, Daphne's ribaldry dispelled it. Notepads and pencils somehow appeared on the bar, as names and telephone numbers were exchanged. Those who had failed to get the target they wanted seized the opportunity for another occasion.

Whether he had been her companion earlier or not, Francis was keeping a close hold on Erika. An arm draped carelessly round her shoulder had a hand that was cupping a breast, his fingers squeezing the nipple. I moved close to and whispered into her ear, "I dare you."

She knew what my dare was.

"Shall I?" she mouthed back. I nodded.

There was a frightened look on his face as Erika persuaded Francis to lie down. She gave his cock a few strokes before standing astride him, her pussy poised directly over his cock. All conversation stopped. Everyone gathered round expecting, as Francis certainly did, that Erika would mount him there and then. Instead, she went into her backbend, gripping her ankles, before letting go with one hand to put his rapidly growing prick into her mouth. It obviously wasn't the first time she'd tasted it. I couldn't imagine Erika kissing a cock that still had someone else's cum stains on it. I moved round so that I could see the position of her cunt, and whether, had Humphrey been erect, I could have slipped him into her. It couldn't be done. Instead, I led the applause.

It was still early evening, and there was general talk about meeting up for dinner, not quite our scene though Erika was included.

"Come back with us. If you want, we'll drop you off, or come in we've got plenty of food in the fridge, we'll cook for you."

Daphne's invitation was reinforced by Dolores. "You may as well, Tony. No point going back to an empty flat."

I wasn't sure it was empty, but the Double Dees were always fun, and I didn't doubt that Humphrey would have recovered by then. It was Dolores who gave him a fondle and felt movement there. She rubbed him against her thigh. "That's settled it. Humphrey wants to come."

"He always does" said Daphne.

Chapter Eleven : Panty Count

Action at the home of the Double Dees was inhibited by the arrival of their parents. His Lordship said he was delighted to meet me, Her Ladyship said they were delighted to meet one of the pupils who would be studying with Daphne and Dolores. The two subjects under discussion meantime were standing in the 'butter in mouth' position, eyes downcast, hands clasped together in front of the apron. The bursar must have been talking to someone. George and the Jaguar were offered me, in addition to many thanks not only for keeping the twins entertained, but for making sure they got home safely!!!

Whoever would have been stupid enough to try to mug the twins would have an experience he would never forget, even when he came out of jail.

I was delighted at being let off the hook. While the twins and their bodies were delectable, the occasional yearning for sleep even crept over me. And this was one of them.

It was dark when I woke. I listened, but could hear no sign of movement in the flat, so I got up, made a cup of tea, turned the taps on in the bathroom and dosed the water with bubble and bath salts. Then of course, I heard the front door close. Deja vu.

It followed exactly the same pattern as that first time, as if THAT had been a rehearsal. All that was missing was the sense of urgency in Mother's movements.

I deliberately didn't make a sound. It was several minutes before the door opened and Mother entered. "Snap. Haven't we played this scene before?" She burst out laughing, and pointed to Humphrey who was making his presence felt, bursting through the bubbles like the conning tower of a Polaris submarine. "Was that in the last production?"

"Yes, but you didn't wait to see him."

"I'm glad to see him now" she said, moving to the bath and bending over to stroke the foreskin up and down, before giving it a kiss on the tip.

"What's the next scene. Oh Yes, I call out to you to close your eyes, and have a quick shower. "Did you close your eyes?"

"No way. I told you. I memorised every bit of you."

It was a very quick shower, and without bothering to dry herself, she joined me in the bath, facing me and then lowering herself gently as I moved Humphrey into position.
She held onto the sides of the bath, letting only Humphrey's head penetrate her, rubbing her clitoris each time. Then, giving a little sigh of relief, she sank dawn and let its full length impale her.

"That's better. That's very much better. Oooh." She held onto the bath and lifted herself up so that only the faintest tip of Humphrey was nudging the lips of her pussy. She moved forward and back on it, teasing herself before lowering herself centimetre by centimetre down its length until she was once more impaled.

"Its so lovely. I could eat it. Was your party any good?"

"Not bad. The Double Dees made quite an effort. Lots of food, some drink but no-one went mad."

"I gather you made another conquest, satin briefs this time."

"You checked my pillow?" I said accusingly.

"Of course, still have to keep an eye on you." "It isn't your eye you've on me now" I said and put my hands under her buttocks to lift them up and down. There was room for my fingers to stroke the sides of her quim as Humphrey slid up and down inside it.

"What was it like at Nan's?"

"Hopeless. For some reason Mother's into men. Suppose it all started with this nudist bit, discovering that her figure's better than most women her age, even ten years younger. She wanted to go out on the pull, so she booked into the Hilton. Didn't take long for a bottle of Krug to be sent across to our table, from, as the waiter said, 'The two Americans over there.'

"They came over to join us, shared it with us, ordered another bottle, and we finished up having dinner. Nightcap of course, and I was with Hank in his room far a brandy while Tom was with Mother. It could have been fine, quite a nice man, but all he wanted was 69. His wife wouldn't suck him, or let him suck her. He was making up for years of deprivation. That's why it was such a relief sinking down on Humphrey, and having him massage me.

"Come on, let's get dried. I want it properly now" she said, getting up, grabbing a towel and holding it out to me. She wrapped it round me as I climbed out of the bath and began drying me. I took another off the rail and gave her body some attention. We were nowhere near dry as we went into her bedroom. We paused only long enough to spread the towels out on her duvet before I was into her. She was wild, I was as bad. It was one of our quickest, first her then me in an orgasmic climax.

We lay, spent, my knee still between her legs, nudging her pussy, for some time. She put her hand under the pillow and found instead of her panties, Ingrid's briefs.

"H'mm" she murmured. "Still damp. This afternoon's."

I admitted they were.

"Whose? I'm not being jealous, just curious. I know you've got a collection of them hidden somewhere, haven't found them yet, but I will. I can't see either of your Double Dees wearing these, they're much more Janet Reger, so these belong to another guest."

"Her name's Ingrid" I said. "She was the P.E. teacher at school. She married a Frenchman, and it was her farewell party." I didn't bother to explain that I now had the use of a flat in London which would be visited by Ingrid and, in due course, her grandson. "A teacher' You've been having an affair with a teacher, a P.E. teacher at that!! What was wrong with the headmistress? I know it happens that men teachers have affairs with girl students, but this is the first time I've heard of it happening the other way round. What sort of school is it I sent you to?

"Do you, er, know many other teachers?"

"One or two. It's just that a lot of the men teachers are wimps, and I'm big for my age."

Mother reached her hand down to Humphrey which was resting on her thigh. She didn't have to say anything. I was big there too.

She made up her mind. "Let's have a look at this knicker collection of yours' Bring them out. We'll put them on the bed."

I kept the pillow slip in a suitcase on top of my wardrobe. When I returned Mother was sitting crass legged on the bed, Ingrid's briefs at one end.

"Have you got them labelled?"

I had to admit I hadn't got around to that yet. "How do you know who's they are?"

"I know them all."

"Oh, do you. I've got some sticky labels. You tell me their names and I'll write them down."

She went to get them. It was rather embarrassing, several panties, as a hand inside the pillowcase proved, were still damp. It was not a good idea for Mother to handle them. She, however, ridiculed my suggestion that I write the labels.

"I know what a pussy smells and tastes like" she said. "I'll wash my hands afterwards." Mother was full of surprises.

Ingrid's label was the first to be applied.

"We'd better keep to the batting order" said Mother. "Who's next?"

I retrieved the garments of the Double Dees from my trainers. "These are Daphnes', and these Dolores'" I collected Mother's panties from the wardrobe. "I know my own" she said, writing 'Jane' on the label.

"Helen" I said, holding out her pants, I'd knotted together those of the girls who'd screwed me on the way to Mother's party and left their knickers in the sports bag. Two of them, those of Daphne and Dolores were doubles, the others belonged to Audrey and Susan, but I didn't know which were which. Those of the Double Dees were easily identified by comparing them with those I brought back today. Mother just took a chance with the other two.

We were coming to my youth, no longer panties but briefs, and before them knickers. I identified them. "Ruth's, we were in the fourth form. We were together all summer, but her father was posted overseas - and she left. June" I said, as Mother held up an exotically patterned brief.

"She was a year older than me, and she saw me in the tub. She had great breasts, most of the girls hadn't got a lot up front, but she loved having them kissed. It was she who taught me about rolling Humphrey between them."

"You're having much better schooldays than I ever had" Mother said bitterly.

"These must be Inge's" she said, producing the pair of white briefs Inge had taken off before initiating me.

"Her letter's on my desk if you want.

The one pair that Mother hadn't asked me to identify were Nancy's purple panties. She wrote a name on a sticker, and showed it to me. It bore the one word, 'Nancy'.

"How did you know?"

"She had a purple set of undies on last night. Then she was talking about this man she'd met with a magnificent penis. The purple panties proved it."

I explained about the earring and how it had been found. "Of course it was no accident, losing that earring. She'd have sacrificed a diamond bracelet to get her hands on Humphrey in his prime. I saw her holding him when I was walking back with the champagne. But don't think you're going to get us both into bed at the same time. I won't allow it."

Chapter Twelve : The Delivery Lady

The phone call could not have been more discreet.

"I wonder if I can have a word with Tony" said the disembodied voice.

"Speaking" I answered, giving nothing away.

"This is Models One. Are you the Tony who had a sculpture done recently?"

It was Joyce. Fat chance I had of joining the skinnies at Models One agency.

"Hi Joyce. 'Tis I. What can I do for you?"

Her voice relaxed immediately.

"Sexy darling. How are you? Listen. I've got the sculptures, remember? Thought you might like to see them before I deliver them to your friend."

Was there a slight emphasis on the word 'friend'? Now what? Having her deliver them to the flat with all the problems that would then follow if Mother saw them was out of the question. But then... St John's Wood. Ingrid's flat. What better Christening of my tenancy?

"Can you be outside here in 15 minutes?" I asked.

"Yes."

"See you."

Joyce was one of those people who needed few words.

Mother I knew, had a disconcerting habit of running through my belongings. It made hiding things from her that much more difficult. The key to Ingrid's flat was on my chain of keys, which included the school bike shed, the pavilion, the gym, changing room, school lab and my room. I took it off the ring.

She had drawn up outside the flats with the near door against the pavement. I was in, and she was off in seconds.

"St John's Wood. Opposite Lords" was all I needed to say.

"Pull over now, bit further. That's fine", was my other addition to the conversation. Joyce was no slouch. Her antennae were tuned to every atmosphere.

She went to the back of her car, but had difficulty in lifting a heavy package. I took it from her, and gave her the key to open the flat. It was a heavy parcel. She had opened the front door and surveyed the flat before I could stagger up the steps into it.

"Well" she said, throwing open the door so that I could drop my burden in the hall. "There aren't many 'O' level schoolboys who have access to a St John's Wood pied-a-terre, as well as their home in town. Don't tell me how it all happened.

"You wouldn't happen to have a glass of something like wine, or beer, lemonade even. It's been a long driving day."

I'd no idea, but I had a faint hunch that Ingrid would have anticipated what her flat would be used for, and left something in the fridge. It was Krug. She was a fan of the Mail diary Editor who would drink nothing else.

Without a word I opened it. She heard the pop, but by that time I had arranged the champagne flutes and was pouring the two glasses.

"Boy" she said, taking one of the flutes and clinking glasses in a silent toast, "What ARE you going to be like in four years time?.

She began exploring the flat. Ingrid had a desk in her sitting room, against the bay window where the light was best.

Joyce went to her bundle and took out the heaviest of her burdens. Plastic bag, tissue paper and there it was. My cock. Twelve and three quarter inches of stainless steel. She stood it on Ingrid's desk, the balls giving it a base to make up over 13 inches altogether.

She ran her fingers up and down it.

"Wouldn't surprise me if a few hundred people are using this to amuse themselves as we speak" she said.

"What few hundred?" I asked.

"My job to tell you" she said. "When I got back with the casts, and we began to run them off, the whole place went wild. It was just what was wanted for all the sex shops in Britain, A genuine twelve-plus incher, uncircumcised, foreskin intact, loves to be handled.

"God knows how many of the plastic ones with batteries, we've sold, but we've sold thousands of the stainless steel ones, "And," she whispered, "we're making one in solid silver for your friend who introduced us."

Joyce was nervous. She wasn't all that good a rep to hide her thoughts.

"Joyce. Joyce, listen to me." She stopped.

"What's the problem? Why are you going on? You could have delivered these without any problems. Why all the fuss?"

"Copyright."

"What? What's copyright got to do with it?"

"Simple. This sculpture was commissioned by your friend. It's her copyright. In the meantime, your cock is now shafting millions of women in all quarters of the globe without a by-your-leave. Our company has turned out millions from that cast. It's the biggest selling item in the world since the crucifix. Your cock is everywhere."

I was beginning to get the drift.

"So ...

"Now they've suddenly woken up to the fact that they've breached your copyright and that of your friend. She in fact, mentioned it to me in a casual phone call, which was not so casual.

"Head office had made a mistake, got caught up with the commercial possibilities and didn't tell me what was going on. But briefly, it seems that in the same way as you commission a photographer to take the photographs, and pay him for them, the copyright is vested with you. You could take them to the cleaners.

"So, as it was my baby to begin with, I've been offered a huge fee to seduce you, so that you accept an offer from them. Then I have to be persuaded to do something similar.

"You mean you've got to seduce me?"

"W..e..e..ll, yes."

I took her by the hand and led her to the bedroom. I stood her beside the bed.

"Now, let me see. Blouse loose." I began by undoing the buttons, and then thought of a quicker way, pulling it out of her skirt, and over her head.

It was there as I'd expected, a lacy half-cup bra which just supported her breasts. I undid it. Her breasts didn't move, they were that firm. I kissed and squeezed them and then stood back. It was her turn. She pulled the tee shirt over my head, and as she had done on the first occasion, dropped to her knees to undo my belt, pull the zip down and take my trousers off, shoes and socks coming off with them.

A hook and eye and a zip brought her skirt down. I knew there would be no panties, just the sexy suspender belt and stockings. She made me stand up and pulled my shorts down. Humphrey was already poised. She pulled me down onto the bed, rolled me onto my back and impaled herself on him.

She braced herself against my legs and began to pump herself up and down.

"D'you know?" she asked, pausing in the ministrations to address herself to the wider fields of things, "there is an international survey taking place now to discover what effect dildos and vibrators have on the relationships between men and women?"

"What's your reaction?" I asked holding my hips still so she got no bounce from them.

"Better than nothing, but you can't beat the real thing and this" she got off me and took Humphrey in her hand, rubbing it against her breasts, taking it in her mouth before climbing back on it, "is the real thing. T just hope I can find enough excuses to come round for a session."

She was too wound up to enjoy sex properly.

"I know I'm going to kick myself tomorrow, but I can't really enjoy it now, I've got to give my company some sort of answer."

I rolled her onto her back, rested her legs on my shoulders and drove into her hard. She gasped as my balls bounced against her bottom and I parted her legs as far as they would go.

"Bastard. You know I can't resist it" she said as she began her orgasm, shouting and screaming, her bottom bucking to meet mine as I fucked her. Afterwards, we rolled onto our sides, she lying still with me deep inside her. I kissed her.

"What sort of deal are you supposed to get me to agree to? What is normal copyright?"

"It depends. Some agents get 20% for their clients, Without even having to apologise for a company error.

I thought for a moment. I'd heard what she was saying. "So, we're in the driving seat. They want to do a deal with us, to their advantage, without any fuss."

"Ye.e.es" she said slowly.

"And they are the guilty party?" "Ye.e.es."

"Then there is only one solution. YOU have to be our agent. We'll get our lawyers to draw it up properly, but in the meantime you can assure the gentlemen outside that YOU speak for us."

The word 'loyalty' was bandied about for a few minutes, until Joyce pointed out that it was only when SHE drew their attention to it, that THEY realized money was owed in copyrights to US.

One million dildos, at £20 each, of which Nancy and I agreed to accept 10% meant £l million for each of us in back payment, not including the regular sums which would continue to be paid into our bank accounts as sales continued.

Nancy, Mother, Joyce, our new agent and I hosted a dinner party in a banqueting room at the Savoy - I was the only male. A11 the girls were there, the Double Dees, Erika, Ingrid and the two girls who once fancied her, Anita and Diana, Helen, Inge who had given me my very first experience, Anita and Diana and others from the past with whom I'd lost contact. Somehow Joyce with Mother's help had traced them all.

Surprise for them all, except Joyce, came with the sweet. As a waiter helped each guest to her choice from the dessert trolley, a waitress placed a full-size Humphrey dildo beside it.

I stood up. "If you want cream" I announced, "turn the base as usual, point it at your pudding and press the button."

There were squeals of delight as cream was ejaculated.

I waited until the laughter had subsided, before adding, "I hope to visit you all personally in time, but until Humphrey can take care of you personally, his replica will be able to take care of your needs."

Erika and I went back to her flat in St John's Wood. Her pregnancy was beginning to show, and it would be our last time together until the baby was born.

"Funny really" she said, kissing Humphrey gently while I caressed her swelling breasts. "As it turned out, we could have got married, you've got enough money to look after us all. Not 17 yet and already a millionaire. Makes this", as she ran her tongue around it, "almost too valuable to use."

Chapter Thirteen : Mother Again

    Almost, but not quite. While she stroked and kissed my cock, keeping me on a slow burn, I kissed every part of her body. Those splendid, full breasts which would be feeding our child got special attention before my mouth made its way down to its main target, her wonderful cunt.

    I wanted to pleasure her rather than share the pleasure, so I slid down the bed.

    "I want to hold it" she moaned, as Humphrey slid out of reach.

    "Later" and I put my mouth to her vulva, my hands slipping under her buttocks to pull her moist pussy to my face. As my tongue found her clitoris and she bucked under me she murmured, "I wonder if there'll ever be a time when you won't find my cunt moist."

    I hoped not, but I didn't pause in my ministrations to say so. Not until she came to her first orgasm did I climb on top of her and let her feed Humphrey into position. She chuckled at the care I took in not pressing down on her stomach.

    "You won't hurt me" she said, pulling me down tight with one arm while the other hand squeezed my balls. "Pump it into me. Let me have every drop of it. Let our baby slide out of me on a cushion of your cum."

It was the most loving fuck I'd had. Ingrid was the girl I loved best, but it was better for her to have a loving husband, and our baby a loving father, while I did my own growing up. At least that was what she told me at the airport the next morning before flying back to Paris. I believed it at the time.

Mother was out when I got home, but Humphrey's replica had pride of place on her bedside table. I wondered whether she had used the substitute while the genuine article was providing a service elsewhere. She had left a number of messages for me and I was reading them when I heard her key in the lock. She swept straight through into my bedroom.

"Darling. You're back. Wonderful."

She sat beside me on the bed and kissed me on the cheek.

"That was some party. Your own harem of sixteen year olds, all getting on together, and not one bitch among them. As for your souvenirs!! Very original."

"I'm glad. Bit cheeky, I know. Have you used yours' yet?"

She pinched my cheek.

"Naughty. That would be telling. But I've only had mine for one day. Haven't had a real chance to try it out."

She became serious. "I take it I'm going to be a grandmother?"

I nodded. "And she's married to someone else who thinks the baby is his?"

I nodded again.

"And she loves you, but married someone else because you're still at school?"

"That's about it."

"I think I rather like my daughter-out-law. I was certainly amused by the rest of your guests. Every one of them could have made me a grandmother, though it would have been intriguing to have sorted out a relationship if Nancy were to have your child."

I wondered what she meant by that remark, but she swept on before I could ask the question.

"Thank God its too late, at least I think it is. Even so it wouldn't surprise me to find she'd gone to some Swiss clinic to have her clock turned back."

"Not that I had any doubts," she continued, "but now its positive you don't fire blanks we'll have to make sure you've got a silencer on your pistol when you fire it."

"Only when it's ready to fire" I replied. "I don't like to feel anything between me and that gorgeous pussy of yours"

The scent of mother's perfume, the feel of her silk dress under my hand, and the glimpse of her breasts as they swelled out was already having its effect. I could feel Humphrey swelling and she sensed it.

"Oh, no" she murmured.

"Oh, yes" I replied as I took her hand and guided it to where my trousers were bulging.

"No" she repeated. "I've got things to do this afternoon, there's lunch..."

I gave her no chance to complete the sentence. With one arm I pulled her back so she lay on the bed, and began a long kiss that had only once conclusion, while the other hand slid between her thighs and began stroking. Her legs parted and I slid my hand up, and under her panties to where her pussy was already moist.

"You're insatiable" she said, as we broke from the kiss. "We'll have lunch later. Now undo my zip while I take care of yours."

Suiting the action to the words, she undid my fly and led Humphrey out through the gap in my boxer shorts into the open. She gave him a few strokes, bent down to give it a kiss before turning so I could undo the zip of her dress. We both stood, me to pull her dress up over her head and then cup and kiss her breasts while she undid my trouser belt and let them drop to my ankles.

As she knelt to remove my shoes, socks and trousers, then pull my shorts down, guiding them gently over the ramrod that was an erect cock, I stripped off my shirt and tie then bent to cup her tits and lift her up by them, turning her so she was lying on my bed. The pose was one I'd photographed several times, she was propped on one elbow, one breast touching the duvet, the other proud and out-thrust, her buttocks curved, lacy panties covering her quim, stocking clad legs crossed at their ankles with a "Now come and fuck me" smile on her face.

I touched her and she fell onto her back, lifting her bottom up so I could peel her panties off. I held them to my nose, then put the juicy crutch into my mouth, before turning my attention to the real thing. Her legs opened to admit me, and then closed firmly on my head as I began nibbling at the little pieces of her bum on either side of her cunt. She let me tease her for a minute before letting me know her wants by pushing my head firmly so my lips met her cunt lips. My tongue found its target as her clit came out to meet it and she began pushing my head down and her hips up in a wild orgasm.

As she relaxed, I was able to breathe through the mask of pubic hair that covered my nose and mouth and moved up the bed so I could kiss her nipples.

"As wonderful as ever" she said, sitting up to kiss me before relaxing once again to let me have my way with her breasts. One hand was playing with her clitoris, squeezing it while other fingers, moist from her juices, gently teased her bum.

I released her clitoris to explore this new situation, while mother rolled onto her side and then onto her front to allow me freedom. My fingers slid as smoothly into that crevice as my cock did with her pussy. It was an entirely new experience for her and she obviously enjoyed it.

"One of my friends has been trying to put his in there, its so tight, but it is getting wider."

"Do you like the feeling?" I asked.

Her voice was muffled, but uncertain. "Ye.e.es, I think so. Have you done it before?"

I remembered Daphne and Dolores, their excitement, and their determination not to do it again, though I expected Daphne to change her mind, judging by her descriptions of it to me.

"Yes, I have."

"With one of the girls at the party?"

"Yes."

"And did they like it?"

"Yes."

All the time, my fingers had been sliding in and out, as far as they would go while her bottom was curved to meet them.

"Put Humphrey there" she asked, and reached for him. We lay like spoons while she held his shaft and guided the big cockhead to its new target. I gave gentle thrusts forward while she pushed back onto it until I felt her bumhole open. She gasped as her sphincter muscles admitted the intruder, and we both paused to let them adjust.

"That's enough" I said.

"No, it feels lovely. Such a full feeling. Play with my cunt" and as I complied, "Oooh,… that is really something. While she was speaking, her bottom was moving as she encouraged Humphrey deeper and deeper inside her.

"Now fuck me, and squeeze my clittie.."

By now, she was on all fours, her bottom raised as high as it would go, while I was on her doggy fashion, one hand squeezing her clitoris, the other caressing her tits. The bed was creaking, she was shouting "Shoot it into me" and I was gasping as, without any apprehension, I shot my load into her arse. Her sphincter muscles milked me just like those in her quim until, limp and empty, my cock slipped out.

We rolled over into the spoon position again and I held her close, cupping a breast in each hand. She snuggled into me.

"That was certainly different. I'm not sure which I prefer."

"Does it hurt?"

"It's a bit sore, but that's because you've got such a big prick."

"You should have waited for your friend to go first."

"His prick is smaller, but I wanted yours to be the first to fuck me there. Now let's both have a bath, we'll soak in it and you can rub some cream into me. Then we'll have brunch."

Chapter Fourteen : The Grandmother

A surfeit is often followed by a drought, and so it happened. After the excitement of finding myself a person of wealth, a father to be, with my own St John's Wood flat, all before I was 17, life went quiet. I concentrated on my lessons at school, interrupted only by a game of rugby and the subsequent bath, with the Double D's making sure I had a clean body to compensate for our dirty minds.

I spent the occasional weekend at home, and it was on one of these that we heard from Nancy. Heard was the word, as the continual sounding of a car horn took mother and me to the window to look down on the street. I already had a suspicion of whose finger was on that button. It was confirmed. She was sitting at the wheel of a Corvette Stingray with its top down. As soon as she saw us she swung her legs over the door, like an American teenager, much to the consternation of some passers by whose hearing had been assaulted by her car horn, and whose eyes were now forced to gaze up a long pair of stockinged legs, the white of her flesh at the top of her thighs and the black panties that concealed where they joined.

I know because she couldn't wait to show us the result of her latest visit to a plastic surgeon, once I'd opened the door to her.

"Wonderful man" she said, lifting up her dress to show her derriere. "Look, not a bit of cellulite" spinning round to give us the benefit of her legs, thighs, and parts of her bush creeping out from her lace panties. "No creases, a smooth bottom just like a page three model. I'll give you his name and address", to mother.

"Thank you, I don't need it" mother replied huffily. I could vouch for that. Mother's bottom was as tight as that of a young boy, the skin smooth with the soft fuzz of a peach. It certainly wasn't suffering from the treatment it was getting.

"Well, you will do one day" said Nancy, matter of factly. "That was only part of what I wanted to show you. Like my car?" she asked me.

I had a suspicion that I'd told her the Stingray was the one I intended to buy one day.

"My favourite car" I had to admit.

"I'll take you for a ride in it, but not now, only a flying visit."

There was a faint sigh of relief from mother, and a lessening in the tension. I wondered if she'd had a bonk in the car, or whether the privilege of Christening it would be mine.

Nancy continued. "The surgeon gave me some advice. He obviously makes lots of money, and he's found ways of keeping it out of the hands of the Inland Revenue. He's got his stashed in the Bahamas, no tax, no nosey parkers, so I've opened accounts there, one for you, and I've arranged for our royalties to be paid into those accounts. Suit you?"

It did.

"And you want to get most of that back payment invested in stocks and shares. There are ways of avoiding tax, by investing in British companies, and these stockbrokers will advise you. They'll ring you and make an appointment for tomorrow."

"But tomorrow's Sunday" I protested.

"I know, but when I told them how much you had to invest they said they'd abandon a holiday for that." What I had to invest was the best part of a million pounds, depending on how much tax could be avoided.

"Must go now. Having lunch with this wonderful man. Odd how many men want to buy you lunch when you're rich enough to be able to pay for them."

With a spin that let her skirt ride up to her waist to give us, me particularly, another sight of the surgeon's skill, she let herself out. It would not be long, I knew, before I would have closer contact with that rejuvenated bottom. Mother knew it also, but she had almost readjusted her thinking to the idea that Nancy was her sister, not her mother.

I opened the window and craned out. Grandmothers of fifty ought not to be driving Stingrays, particularly when they were left hand drive. If they did own one, they ought to be chauffeur driven, or at least they should open the door to get in and out of the car, not sit on the edge and swing their legs over, displaying everything from ankles to ass.

Nancy did, even giving us a wave with her legs before sliding down into the seat, starting the car and burning rubber as she set off.

"What sort of tablets can she be taking" murmured mother as she closed the window and reset the burglar alarm.

We resumed positions in our chairs, and she adopted her mother's mien.

"Well, what do you think?"

"Looks alright, but the stitches are bound to show if you get close enough. Anyway, YOU don't need any nips and tucks now."

"Don't be stupid" she said, stretching out a leg so her toe rested, threateningly, on my balls. "Sensible talk. What do you think of her idea of investing your money?"

"What do YOU think?" I replied. "It isn't just my money."

"It IS just your money. I'm certainly not going to insist that you do nothing without my approval. You do what you like with it, you're sensible enough not to get into drugs and things. Nancy may not know much about investing money, but.." I chimed in with the rest of the saying, "She knows a man who does." Nancy always did.

"But before she goes any further, your Father has to be consulted.

"My Father? Why?"

It was seldom he came up in conversation. Nothing had ever been said, but I'd always had the impression that he'd treated mother badly and they'd split as a result.

Mother in fact took the call from the stockbroker's office.

"He obviously likes his Sunday lunch" she said, looking at the notes she'd made. "His secretary suggested four o'clock, which means we can have lunch, then I'll get out of the way and leave you to it. You can tell me all about it afterwards. L.S. Powell's his name. However, I'll bring your Father up to date with events. He might decide to be there with you."

Surprise, surprise. Apart from the fact that he'd been awarded a baronetcy by Blair, nothing I was particularly proud of though it would make me a 'Sir' in due course, I'd no idea what my father did. I might learn a bit more tomorrow if he decided to attend the meeting with the stockbroker. I rather hoped he would.

Saturday was mother's night for bridge, while I usually spent a few hours either working out or demonstrating at Erika's health centre. It depended on events whether one of the students or Erika came back to St John's Wood with me. I always left mother with a clear field at home. The bridge club was filled with her suitors and sometimes one was invited home for coffee ...and whatever.

Since our introduction at the Double D's party Erika and I had become friends as well as, often, lovers, indeed

177

we were now partners. Her initial backer had pulled his money out, because he found he wasn't getting the attention from her that he wanted. She was telling her staff the bad news when I found out. The first royalty cheque from 'Hard Timers', the company making the dildo, bought me a 49% share. I wanted to leave Erika as the boss.

That evening, she shooed the clients away, including the dark, South American girl, roughly my own age, whose work-out I'd been supervising. Her leotard barely covered her boobs, and while it nipped into her waist adequately, so many of her dark, curly, pubic hairs were visible that I was contemplating trimming then with scissors when Erika tapped my shoulder.

"She'll be back again. She's on a six week course. St John's Wood or here?"

I stood up from where I'd been sitting on the Mexican girl's ankles while she thrust the bar and its weights upwards.

Her tawny breasts were cascading out of her leotard, and I'd been wondering at what point I should pull the garment down to her waist, and let her breasts escape, probably into my lips.

"That's enough" I said, making sure the bar was resting in its notches. I moved round to her shoulders and began pulling her out from under the press. As luck would have it, her leotard got caught and as I pulled her up, it stayed down leaving her naked to the waist.

They were as good as I'd imagined, and it was not imagination to see that her nipples were excited, thrust out, as proud as they would ever be.

Unconcerned, she swung her legs over and sat up. Without hurry, she pulled the leotard over her shoulders. The act of tucking each breast inside would have brought a round of applause at any strip club. "Next week?" she asked.

I made a hurried check through my mental diary. "Next week" I agreed. The date had been made. We all watched her make an unhurried departure, the wonderful globes of her bottom separated only by the cotton of the leotard, clinging tightly to the crease between her muscular buttocks.

Erika let me take my fill before grabbing my arm. "Come on you lecher. It's only seven days to next week and you'll have enough on your hands, and other parts, with me. I'll get Benjie to lock up. I DO need to talk with you."

It HAD to be serious before Erika would get that concerned.

"Taxi?" I asked.

"At the door."

"Right. let's go."

I poured a large brandy for her, a bottle of cider for myself while waiting for Erika to change. There was always a selection of dressing gowns in the linen cupboard for girls to wear once they'd decided to stay. Erika had chosen a Paisley, cotton one, which brought out the lights in her auburn hair, but with the belt loosely tied, her figure was revealed as she moved.

I let her pick up the brandy goblet before taking her hand and pulling her over to me.

"Well?" I asked, as I undid the dressing gown belt and lifted up a breast to my mouth.

She let me fondle and kiss each breast before saying, "Stop it Tony. I want to talk to you seriously, and I can't while you're turning me on. Lift your head up."

I obliged, but continued massaging her wonderful breasts and her long legs.

"What is it that can take precedence over a long, lingering fuck, which I propose giving you?"

"I've had an offer for the Health Centre." That did bring me up short. I had thoughts of protection racketeers, muscle heavies beating up the lovely people I knew at the centre.

I must have shown my thoughts on my face and as I asked, "Genuine or funny people?." She began laughing. "Oh genuine, quite genuine. Its the tennis player who has the tennis and fitness school at Isleworth. He wants to expand, include tennis coaching at our centre and let me carry on as manager."

"Would you want that?"

"Oh Yes. I could pay you back the money you've put in and that would still leave me enough to buy a place of my own, and have a better than schoolteacher's income."

"That's it then. Do it" I said, bending down again to take one of her nipples in my teeth and biting it.

"Is that all you've got to say?."

"What else is there? It's your place and if it suits you, it suits me. But don't let it go until after next week."

"Why not until then? Oh, of course, you wretch," grabbing my goolies and squeezing them. "The Mexican girl. Pig. She'll still be there, and I'll still be running it so you can take your pick of the members, Now taste these", saying which she pulled my head down to her breasts.

I didn't tell her that I'd signed my shares in the centre over to her. Had we both been four years older, me 20 and she 27, we could well have been married. But then, so could Ingrid and I. And a few others, I reflected, lifting her up and carrying her into the bedroom.

Erika busied herself in the kitchen the next morning. She loved preparing breakfast, and one of the things I did do was to keep the fridge full of food, and Krug. I got up. put my dressing gown on, took the champagne out of the fridge, lifted up Erika's dressing gown and rubbed the cold bottom against her bumcheeks before bending down to kiss them.

"Uum, that's nice" she said wriggling, as I kissed the cleft, and then jumped as I thrust the cold bottle top into her very wet pussy.

"Careful, or I'll pour this pan on you" she warned, holding the pan of bacon above my head.

"You wouldn't", but then I knew she might. So, taking no chances, I stood up, opened the bottle, took a carton of orange juice from the fridge and combined the two.

Chapter Fifteen : The Money Broker

Mother knew I wouldn't be home for Sunday lunch and had joined some friends, leaving me to a leisurely breakfast and a rumpty tumpty with Erika. I was definitely a boobs person, firm ones with nipples that stuck out, or even up. Erika's were in that category. She also had the advantage of long straight legs, delightfully curved, slim ankles, the sign of a real thoroughbred and a pussy which I delighted in eating, with or without salt. Having charged my batteries, ready for a boring discussion about money and stocks and shares with Mr L.S. Powell, I called a cab, dropped Erika off at the health centre, and went home.

I'd had another four hours sleep, and a leisurely shower by four o'clock. Punctuality was obviously a creed with Powell. The clock hadn't stopped chiming when the doorbell rang. I had a last look around, mother had prepared the dining table for the conference and had equipped it with notepaper and pens.

I was expecting a dried up money-man, probably an ex-income tax inspector, gamekeeper turned poacher, about fifty, the sort of man every bank keeps in its cupboard. I couldn't have been more wrong. I opened the door to an L.S. Powell who was, in fact, a power dressed, straight above the knee skirt which hugged her buttocks, and matching jacket, seamed stockings, court shoes, frilly see-through blouse showing a lacy bra, a gorgeous sex symbol.

They must have combed all their offices to find a girl with these looks and class.

"Mr Cole please" she asked, looking beyond me to where my older brother or father might be.

"That's me" I replied, holding the door open for her to enter.

That really got to her.

"You're Anthony Cole? The one I've come to advise on how to invest a million pounds?" Her voice broke on the words pounds.

"The one and only" still holding the door open. "Won't you come in?"

She caught herself.

"Thank you" and took the three paces that brought her into the flat. I closed the door. Her back view with the skirt cutting under the cheeks of her bum, no panty line, was equally tempting.

"Please, sit down" I said, leading her to the dining table and holding out a chair for her.

"Would you like a drink of some kind, tea, coffee. perhaps you'd like a gin and tonic, you look as if you've had a surprise."

"I'd love a gin", she said with a rueful smile. "It has been a surprise. I was expecting a much older man."

"I was expecting a much older man too", I observed, pouring her drink and just a tonic for myself.

"Finding a beautiful girl was going to advise me on how to invest money is quite a change. Beautiful girls normally advise me on how to spend it."

"I can do that too" she said, taking the glass from me. "Part of my character. I'm a Gemini." "At least it won't be money wasted" I replied. Her grin grew wider. "Old world charm in a young man. Thank you kind sir. Now this is the boring bit." From her briefcase she produced a number of booklets and pamphlets which she spread out.

"Do you really have a million pounds to invest?" giving me a quizzical look. She wasn't sure where to place me. Either I was old beyond my years, or I had a Dorian Gray type portrait hidden in an attic.

I went through mother's room into my bedroom and found the letter from 'Hard Timers' notifying me that a cheque for that amount was waiting for me, needing only the name of the account to which it should be sent. "Phew" she said and turned her chair so that she could sit at one side to the table, and cross her legs. She'd made up her mind. I was old beyond my years.

I replenished her glass, a quick eyelash flutter as a 'Thank you' and moved my own chair so I could give her legs my full attention. She made no comment, but continued turning over the pages, marking paragraphs in the document she was reading.

Stockings or tights, I wondered, and looked for the tell-tale sign of the suspender buttons. There wasn't one, but I made a mental bet with myself that she was a stockinged girl.

"Stockings" she said, reading my mind. "Were you right?"

I nodded. "Yes. But you threw me, I couldn't see any trace of suspenders."

"Garters" she said, pulling her skirt up to reveal the red garters clasping her black stockings to her thighs. She gave me a glimpse of white thigh before she pulled the skirt down, re-arranged it and re-crossed her legs.

"Now that's enough about my clothes, let's get on with my reason for being here. I take it this money was an inheritance and that you want to invest it so it provides an income for you and your family?"

"Not really, I said. "I earned it and there are royalties coming in regularly, but they'll be going straight to the Bahamas, a bank there."

"Sensible. So you must be a pop star, though your face isn't familiar."

Not my face, I thought, but you might recognise another portion of my anatomy. I made no reply.

"Do I call you Tony or Anthony. Mr Cole seems much too formal."

"I'm usually Tony. What are you, Lesley?"

"No, Lois. Would you mind if I took my jacket off? These mansion flats are so warm."

"Of course not. I'll get a hanger."

As I got one from my wardrobe, I had the wild idea that I could get into this girl's knickers. I was certain of it when I took the jacket from her. There had been only one button undone on her blouse, I'd noticed it particularly. Now there were two, part of her lacy bra was visible. It looked as if it provided decoration more than support. Her nipples were pouting against the silk of her blouse. Money was the greatest aphrodisiac.

I let her put the coat on the hangar but made no move to take it from her. I wanted to see her reaction when she went into my bedroom.

"Hang it in my room. Its through mother's."

She could hardly miss the life-sized silver dildo that had pride of place on my dressing table. How would she react?

She hadn't missed it and there was a thoughtful look on her face as she returned. She tucked her blouse firmly into her skirt before resuming her seat. The tightened blouse accentuated the shape of her breasts even more.

"That's a funny thing you've got on your dressing table" she said, putting some papers on the table in front of me. "If you don't mind my saying so, it looks like a giant dildo."

"That's just what it is" I replied.

"I see. So that's what it is" she mused. She'd taken her shoes off and was wiggling her toes.

"Let me" I said, squatting on the floor and picking up her foot before she could protest. I loosened the stocking from around her toes and began massaging them one by one, pulling them so they cracked. Then I stroked the sole of her foot until she pulled it away.

"Now the other one."

Without protest she put her other foot in my hand. "Its better without stockings."

For answer, she lifted her skirt, pulled the garter up so it no longer held the stocking and began peeling it off. Before it got to her knee I took it from her and rolled it down and off her foot. She reached up for the garter and pulled it down, surrendering it to me as it got to her knee.

"It would be like a tourniquet there" she said.

I began massaging her bare leg from the knee down, pulling each toe when I got to her foot. Then I raised it to my mouth and began nibbling them with my teeth.

I could see up her legs to the purple panties that hid her pussy.

"Wonderful." You can do that all day" she said, lifting her other leg and putting it into my lap. She could obviously feel my hardened cock, and began stroking it with her toes through my trousers, moving the leg still with the stocking on, into my hands. She made no attempt to remove the garter so I lifted her skirt up and ran my hands up her leg. A hiss of pleasure escaped her lips as I reached the garter and pushed it up, past the stocking top, onto the bare flesh of her cool thigh.

    I left my hands there for a moment, feeling the moist warmth of her cunt against my fingers. Slowly, I eased the stocking down, peeled it off her foot, and let it resume its old position in my crutch. Her toes began massaging my cock at once.

    She was still worrying about the dildo.

    "But why've you got a dildo in your room. Seems like its silver. Is it?"

    I reached up for the garter, still round her upper thigh, and gently stroked her pussy with the back of my hand. It was damp. She moved it away, but made no protest. I made a production of pulling the garter down, placing it alongside its fellow and licking her cum juice off the back of my hands before turning my attention to these toes.

    "Yes, its silver. It was a presentation" I said taking her toes out of my mouth.

    "But what for?"

    She was now slouched down in the chair, her skirt well above her waist. She was already creaming. I put both her feet down beside me, knelt up and gradually pulled her skirt down.

"It's too tempting" I said piously. "I'm only human."

"So'm I" she said, her hands undoing her waistband, then pulling her skirt down and over her feet. She slid down, next to me on the floor, making her pussy available to me. I began finger-fucking her, sliding them under the crutch of her panties and into her pussy lips until I found her clitoris.

"But why did they give YOU a presentation?", lying back, almost purring as my fingers stroked her cunt. "Because I posed for it. Its a copy of my penis." She lay still, taking in this remark, then relaxed as the obvious explanation came to her.

"You mean they took photographs of it, then enlarged them up and someone made a mould or something?"

"No, they made a mould directly from my cock." She gave a squeal, jumped to her feet and, little buttocks bouncing, rushed into my bedroom.

"You mean this", dumping the silver casting on the floor between us, "is how big your cock is?"

"Yes" I answered calmly, picking up her feet again, continuing the massage, now moving my hands upwards until her smooth thighs were in my hands. Almost unconsciously, she moved her bumcheeks forward within range of my fingers as they reached for the top of her panties.

I pulled them off, and pulled her so she was pillowing her head on my thigh.

"Would you like to see it?" I asked, slipping two fingers inside her cunt-lips and caressing her clitoris.

It was a whispered 'Yes'"

"Then why don't you find it?" I asked, undoing my belt and wriggling my trousers down over my hips. She helped me get them past my legs and feet. Humphrey was still concealed by my boxer shorts. "Go for it" I said.

"Not if it's really as big as this. It would split me. Yet you're only a boy."

"Wait until I'm a man" I answered, taking her hand.

I knelt up, leaving Lois to support herself on her elbows, her eyes fixed on my crutch, the juices on her pussy hairs catching the light as I pulled my shorts down to my knees.

"My God. Its true" she said as Humphrey sprang into freedom. She recoiled as his tip came within a fraction of smacking her.

She sat up and watched as it gradually took position against my belly. Her fingers fumbled with the buttons of her blouse until her tits were swinging in front of her. Then in a curious shuffle on her knees, she brought them up to

Humphrey and rolled his glans between her breasts, taking her nipples up and down his length.

"That's wonderful. How come you've got a cock like this", rubbing its purple head in the valley between her tits before taking a deep breath, kissing its tip and then taking it into her mouth.

She sucked it for a few minutes before saying, "I've got enough trouble getting it into my mouth, never mind into my honeypot."

She pulled the foreskin back and rubbed the smooth cheek of the glans against her face, before kissing it, then slipping it into her mouth again.

"Will it hurt?" she asked, putting Humphrey between her thighs, but making sure his tip didn't get to her pussy lips.

"You'll make room for him. There'll be plenty of room. You'll soon be asking if there isn't a bigger one. Try it."

I stripped and lay on the carpet. Humphrey ready to play his game of 'tents'.

She grasped it and guided it to where her cunt was moist with her juices. She needn't have worried. Humphrey slid in with only a gasp of surprise from her as she spread her legs to their widest extent to accommodate him.

"Mmmmm" she muttered into my ear as she bounced up and down on him before rolling so I was on top. No sooner had I got adjusted to the new position than she doubled herself right back, her feet touching the floor behind her. It gave us the deepest ever penetration which Humphrey and I took advantage of. The tip of my cock must have been stroking her kidneys.

"This is the best Sunday afternoon I've ever had" she said, before her voice rose into "I'm coming. I'm coming. I've come."

The last words came out in a scream as she bucked and bounced underneath me. There was no doubt that she'd orgasmed. Her body jerked, her vaginal muscles gripped as if they would never let go, her heels were raking my back and her teeth were sunk in my neck. "Sorry about that" she murmured, as blood from the bites dripped onto her breasts. She gave me a shove, and I, obediently, rolled off her.

"Thanks" she said, her hand reaching for Humphrey and beginning a slow wank.

"Now you. It's safe. I'm on the pill." I made no move to climb back onto her.

"Or would you rather..." She rolled onto her stomach, her breasts on my thighs while she guided Humphrey towards her mouth. I didn't need to signal assent. Her lips closed on the tip, and her tongue began ringing the rim. I let Humphrey off the leash and he responded nobly.

It might have been the biggest cock her lips had closed on, but she was an expert. For thirty minutes she took me round the Garden of Eden, I never knowing whether it was her hands or her lips on my cock or balls until she decided I could come.

"Jeezus, its growing bigger" she shouted as he pumped everything he had into her.

As his ejaculations died away she rolled off me. We lay on our backs, side by side, my hand cupping her cunt, hers holding a temporarily limp and subdued Humphrey.

"Even now he's bigger than some I've had. What do you call him, Supercock?"

"No, just Humphrey."

"I'll remember that. Can I call on him again." "Fraid you'll have to. We didn't get much paperwork done. It's Humphrey who made me a millionaire, royalties on all the copies of him."

"I see. Well, at least I've had a touch of the real thing though I'll have to get myself a copy for when I feel lonely."

Chapter Sixteen : 'Tony's Secret Weapon'

Of course it was one of the waitresses at our little celebration party who tipped the tabloids off. 'The Teenage Tiger'. 'Tony's Secret Weapon', 'Scuse me, I've Got Something in My Throat' were the milder headlines. The Sun used a photograph of the dildo to make it's headline '£ove you, course I £oves you, I £icks you, don't I?"

No-one bothered about the change of consonant. The Press Commission on intrusion very quickly laid down that, as a sixteen year-old schoolboy, I could not be interviewed without my mother being present. Wisely, she declined. However, with no alternative, the cameras focused on her and Nancy, my co-partner. Both turned out to be natural personalities. Within months mother became a regular feature on quiz shows, having made a name on programmes which discussed precocious children. Her youth, looks and long legs, were a favourite of the TV cameramen, who found it difficult[to train their cameras on less attractive participant.

Nancy, who by now looked little older than her daughter, had become the example by which all grandmothers were judged. She hosted a programme advising the elderly how to enjoy life. She was such a bundle of energy herself that on the principle of 'I'll have what she has', a number of unfortunate grandfathers found themselves badgered into withdrawing their life savings from the bank, so that their spouse could set out on a course which would let them look like Nancy.

The only sufferer was me. Each morning, a queue of teenage girls formed outside the flat, waiting to see me. They had started forming at 2-0a.m. the caretaker told us, the day after the tabloids struck. When I first looked out of the window I was horrified seeing the parade of nubile young crumpet, sitting on the steps and pavement, their little bottoms catching all sorts of chills.

It was a problem for Joyce, our agent. Her formula was simple. Within two hours she had found a thousand autographed photographs of me and was going down the line, giving one to each girl. To the occasional one she gave an address label with a whispered instruction to write to that address with a recent photograph.

The following day's reporting of the fans referred to them as 'Tony's Cock-sparrers' a term which stuck.

I hid out, using the St John's Wood flat when I was home from school. I was sipping a glass of Krug, courtesy of Ingrid's order, going through some of the letters and photographs sent by my fans, wondering whether to get them together for a wild orgy, or take them one at a time, when I heard the high-pitched scream, of a motor-cycle. These two-strokes DO make a noise, but this was something else.

As I looked down from a bay window, I saw the motor-bike appear on the pavement. Then, at the last moment, a figure detached itself, rolled, head tucked into its body, until it was brought to rest by my gate pillar. As it scrambled to its feet, and came running up the steps to pound on my door I could hear the police sirens. Even as I opened it, I knew who my visitor was, and it only spelled trouble. It pushed past me and rushed to the window.

Through the partly open door I saw a stream of police cars and motor cycles speed past.

"Quick" said the figure, tearing off her helmet to reveal Dolores, "jam the door open." She looked with disdain at the antique furniture in the hall and dining room, measuring a line from the front door. "Give me a hand to move these."

We had barely got the hall and dining table moved against the wall, when the motor-cycle sounded its progress.

"Get out of the way, and be ready to close the front door" commanded Dolores.

As I took up position, I saw the motor-bike mount the pavement across the road, turn until it was facing my front door. The rider opened her throttle, I knew who was driving, let in the clutch and bounded off the kerb, across the road, picking up speed, up the other kerb and straight up the steps into my front door.

I closed it immediately, even before Daphne, it had to be her, had cut the engine.

The police sirens approached, and then died. "Shit" said Daphne, her helmet off and stripping off her leathers to reveal her normal casual gear, bra and panties. "I thought I'd lost them."

We crowded the windows, careful not to disturb the lace curtains. Police cars were still arriving. Two motor-cyclists sat on their machines while questions were fired at them,

"They'd love to do a house to house search, but no-one's going to stand for that in St John's Wood" said Daphne, bestowing a French kiss on me me as I handed her a glass of champagne. "Certainly not for a motoring offence,.. or two" adding an afterthought.

"And all this because we wanted to discuss an idea we had." She waved an arm to the tyremarks on the carpet and the motorbike which was making strange noises as it cooled.

"But it doesn't matter. It'll have to stay here for a week or two, until they get fed up looking for it, but as you won't be here who cares?" She waved her arm langorously.

I'd no idea that I wasn't going to be here. But, with the Double D's, one played the cards as they fell. One lunch-time invitation had turned out to be the sexiest weekend of my life. Nevertheless, forewarned is forearmed.

"What was all this business with police about?" I asked.

"These coppers can't take a joke" said Daphne, her tongue firmly in her cheek. "There was this traffic light breakdown at Hyde Park corner with a bobby controlling the traffic. I drew up alongside him to ask the way, and as he was directing me, Dolores cut his belt. The weight of his truncheon, his radio and so on pulled his trousers down. He was screaming, waving his arms and jumping up and down as we drove off, and of course the traffic misunderstood. It was chaos.

"Then we saw these police bikes outside a cafe so we squeezed some superglue on the saddles, turned their mirrors round and sent rude messages on their phones. They've been chasing us ever since, but they can't get off their bikes."

"Then there was the police car. He was hiding out in the Euston Road waiting for someone to make a mistake at a zebra crossing. Daphne drew up alongside and I slapped one of these big, sticky, 'Don't park here again' sheets over the driver's side of the windscreen."

"An interesting morning" I commented wryly. "You could easily have hurt yourselves. Now what do I do with a motor-bike in my sitting room"?

"Nonsense" said Daphne. "We'd been practising that roll and that climb up the stairs for weeks. Nothing was ever going to go wrong. No, what we've come to do is take you out of it, take you abroad so you're not bothered by any cock-sparrers - at least not by any strange ones. Now listen."

It certainly would be exciting. Excitement lay in wait for the twins in staid London, what it would have in store for them motor-cycling through the Continent was anybody's guess. The essence of it was that, at 16 we could get a licence to drive a 125cc bike. The twins already had passed their tests, and I would have to hurry up, learn to ride a bike, take a test and buy one. No problem. Then, with a minimum of luggage on the panniers we would spend three weeks touring, staying on camp-sites, youth hostels or whatever hotels would admit us. We could easily afford the best and though good hotels would be unlikely to admit us in leathers and helmets, I determined to try them. Destination: South of France.

South-east to be exact, the Canal du Midi on which I'd spent a week sailing on a barge, well away from everything. It gained approval from the twins.

We raided Ingrid's wardrobe to find clothes for the Double D's, they certainly couldn't leave in their leathers.

It was two weeks before the police withdrew their 24- hour watch and we were able to man or rather woman handle, the bike down the steps, into the street, in the early hours. We wheeled it a mile before Daphne started it and rode off, just in case a busybody neighbour saw which house it left.

I made a protest about taking leathers and boots when we were going to such a warm climate, but I was over-ruled. Leathers, I was assured, were essential.

The twins, as it turned out, knew the market much better than I.

The motor-cycle course, which pronounced that I was fully qualified to ride a 125cc machine, was also able to find an early date for me to take my test. The result was that two leather clad riders pulled up outside mother's flat, their full-face helmets concealing their faces. Equally hidden by a helmet, I left the flat, picking my way down the cock-sparrers, to join them.

I waited until I'd undone the padlock which kept the machine chained up, put it in the pannier and kick-starting my machine into life before lifting my helmet for a moment. As the 'Sparrers' spotted me, I pulled the helmet down, engaged gear and roared off after the D's. No point leaving the Sparrers watching an empty house. At least mother would have a clear entrance to her flat for the first time in months.

While we all had different machines, mine a Honda, the twins riding a Suzuki and a Kawasaki, they'd all gone through the hands of George, the Double D's chauffeur who knew how to 'improve' motor-cycle engines.

The ride to Dover gave us the first chance to try them out. On the downhill run into the port itself I touched eighty, with the twins hot on my tail. That, I thought, was fast enough for a light-weight bike with narrow tyres, that would skeeter about on hitting a matchstick.

Once ashore and through immigration, we headed straight for Paris. I'd phoned Ingrid to tell her we were coming, much to her husband's delight who had planned on enjoying one of the twins at his 'Farewell to England' party. He'd missed out, but Erika had more than compensated. Now he had a second chance while I renewed acquaintance with Ingrid and her son.

The twins didn't bother to ring doorbells. They announced our arrival by performing 'wheelies' outside the house, in which I had to join, narrowly missing each other in an act that would have impressed a Royal Tournament audience.

Ingrid and Francis led the applause as we switched our engines off, chained the bikes up and followed them into the house. There was no standing on ceremony.

"Champagne or bath" said Ingrid, holding an opened bottle of Krug in one hand and glasses in the other, while in the distance we could hear the sound of running water.

"Both" the three of us said, almost in unison as we peeled off our leathers and scampered to where Francis had filled the tub. With a bit of rearranging of limb positions, it was big enough to accommodate three and we sat soaking while Ingrid refilled our glasses.

As usual, the twins set the pace. They stood up, handed their glasses to Ingrid then passed the soap and sponge to Francis.

Nothing loath, he set to bathing them with gusto, paying special care to their naughty bits until both girls were wriggling.

I seized the opportunity to slip out of the bath, into a welcoming towel held by Ingrid who led me to the nursery. Our son, Francis Anthony, two months old, was fast asleep. At least I'd seen him.

We tiptoed away and were back in the sitting room, me wrapped in a towel when the others joined us. Francis, with two girls to dry, didn't know where to start. Daphne had resolved it by giving him two towels, one for each girl. He did his best, drying each pair of buttocks, then getting caught by the next pair and then the breasts which overshadowed him.

"Enthusiastic, but probably lacking in staying power" Dolores whispered in aside to me" as she moved across to

Francis and covered his nether regions with her towel. Daphne joined them.

Ingrid got up, took my hand and led me to the second bedroom where our son lay sleeping. She slipped out of the housecoat she had been wearing, and nudged me so that I fell onto the bed, my towel dropping off in the process.

"Better you on the outside" she said, turning to me, and as I took up position to mount her, she moved so that one of her knees was pressed against her crutch.

"Kissee no fuckee" she said, squirming her pussy against my knee, her breath hard against my ear.

"Kiss my nipples. I want you to taste my milk. Francis Anthony is waiting to be fed. You can give it to him. Lift him gently."

He was only a morsel, but when I lifted him from his cot and passed him to his mother, he fastened his mouth on the nipple mine had just left as if there was a milk shortage.

"Just like his father" Ingrid chuckled. "And something else. They wanted to circumcise him, but I refused to have him touched. Fortunately the doctor agreed. His cock he said, was too big to be cut."

"How old are they when they cut them?"

"Three months."

"And Francis Anthony was less than two months old?"

"Like Father like son" she said, unglueing our son from one breast to the other. Having fed, burped and changed the baby, Ingrid rejoined me in the bed.

"That, my sweet" she said quite seriously, her back turned to me "is as close as you're going to get to your son. From now on, you'll be Uncle Tony. That is, if you want to see him at all. "

"I'll be Uncle Tony."

She turned over and took my face in her hands, holding herself close against me.

"I will tell him, one day."

"No don't ever. He's got a good family."

"I'll bring him to England in a few months. I'll be O.K. then. I had to have some stitches, and you're much too big. Now you'd better go, the others will be flinging Francis out soon."

She was right. As I looked into the other bedroom, he was just on the vinegar strokes, pumping up and down with extreme gusto, though the casual wave Dolores gave me indicated he wasn't doing her much good.

There was no sign of Daphne. I found her lounging on a sofa in the sitting room, welcoming me with open arms, and legs. Humphrey, who had become a bit comatose, perked up at once, and Daphne used him to pull herself up into a sitting position.

"Here, you lie down."

I obeyed, and she took up a position, her legs stretched out on either side of me, feet towards my face. I took her hands in mine and pulled her forward so that she was in position, supporting herself with one hand while she found Humphrey with the other. Gradually she lowered herself until his cockhead was touching her clit.

"That's better" she smiled. "These long rides sitting on a motor-cycle saddle do give you an appetite. Better than riding horses. No wonder so many policewomen want to be motor-cycle cops." She pulled herself up and down, not letting Humphrey go in any further than her pussy lips.

"I used to slip the clutch and give the throttle another few thousand revs just to feel the lovely vibration on my clitty. Now!"

She let go my hand and lowered herself so that his entire length was inside her. Then, having slipped a hand down to make sure my balls were tucked safely between my thighs she grasped my hands and began a most momentous fucking that brought Dolores and Francis in to watch.

"Alors" said Francis in admiration, as Daphne paused at the top of a stroke revealing Humphrey's size. Dolores seized the opportunity to grasp it and waggle it against her sister's pussy, even moving it out of alignment.

"Put it back" Daphne urged. "I'm getting ready." She was too. I felt like a rower on the Thames as she used my strength to pull herself up and down on her cock, her big breasts bouncing against each other, the cheeks of her bum squelching as they made contact with my thighs, wet from her juices. The strokes became quicker and quicker until she burst out in a scream that brought Ingrid into the room.

"He has such a massive preek." her husband whispered to her.

"Look" he pointed to where Humphrey was revealed, wet and steaming, as Daphne's orgasm ended.

"Yes, it is lovely and big" Ingrid answered, adding as Francis gave her a glum look, "but this" taking his limp little prick in her hand, "is my favourite."

He cheered up, but became downcast again as Dolores straddled me, knees on either side, and began bouncing. His efforts had obviously not been enough for her.

I was able to use my hands to support and fondle her breasts, replicas of her sister's, as she built up steam, but it was Daphne who provided the finishing touch. She disappeared into the kitchen, and after a few moments came back with a slim candle about six inches long. I knew instantly what she was going to do.

She wet it with her mouth and as Dolores made an up stroke, positioned it next to my penis. Dolores, aware of developments, lowered herself gently until her bumhole was on the candle, there was a slight pause before the candle went in and Dolores began her orgasm.

Chapter Seventeen : Boobs Fore & Aft

It wasn't the first time I'd woken up with one beautiful face in front of me and one behind, one pair of firm boobs nudging my chest and another pair at my back. But I never got tired of it. I moved a fraction and Daphne opened her eyes. It was usually Daphne's face I woke up to. Considering our youth, it was surprising how often I did wake up between the Double D's.

She smiled, leaned forward to kiss me on the lips, then burrowed down in the bed so her head was on my chest and her hand holding Humphrey. Though the twins shared me when we were together, they'd come to an agreement, without mentioning it to me of course, that I'd come inside them in turn. So that if the contraceptive devices failed, they would fail on both girls. They'd thus be able to share the costs.

The situation hadn't arisen so I'd not had to disclose what my position would be, though I suspected baby or not, I'd finish up marrying Daphne - unless Ingrid became free in time.

We left our leathers with Ingrid. They were too hot for Paris, and where we were going it was even warmer so it was shorts and sweatshirts. Though the twins called me a prude, I insisted they wore panties under their shorts. They balked at panties, but agreed on bikini bottoms which itself created a crisis, their pubes had grown out of their bikini line, and very obviously, were creeping out at the sides.

Francis donated his electric razor and clippers and watched with interest as the girls lay on their backs, legs astride me while I gave their pussies a short back and sides, taking great care not to trim the naughty bits.

Ready at last, we set off for the south, the twins already gathering attention in their short shorts, sweatshirt which allowed their breasts full movement, and white cowboy boots.

It was inevitable that we should acquire an outrider escort of motor-cycle cops on big BMWs that escorted us to the outskirts of Paris before waving us down, checking our papers giving us a salute and waving us on.

It must have been a quiet day in the TV newsrooms, because camera crews turned up to interview us. We didn't mind. Three British teenagers going to the South of France were following a well-trodden path. What I didn't expect was that a smart French TV reporter would connect my name, not with my millionaire status in England, but with my Father who was now the British Defence attache in Paris.

Fortunately, he discovered that after we were well on the way South, but it didn't stop him including the item in the piece he wrote for Paris Soir. Which, in turn was read by my father, who asked for a recording of the interviews.

It wasn't too difficult for Sir Anthony Cole of Her Majesty's Government to keep tabs on the whereabouts of three young British motor-cyclists riding down to the south of France. And as I learned later, that is exactly what he did.

We'd chosen a village called Vendenac, in a wine growing area on the Canal du Midi and had already booked a Gite big enough for the three of us. Great as a base, where the bikes could be left safely while we explored.

We were having our first breakfast, hot croissant, butter, marmalade and pots of coffee on the patio the following morning, when a taxi drew up.

"Can you spare another cup of coffee?" asked my father, having paid the cab driver and walked towards us.

Daphne was the first to spot the resemblance and was on her feet in a second.

"One coffee coming up. Sugar and milk?"

"Just black please Daphne, or is it Dolores?"

"Daphne" I answered for her, standing up and greeting him with a handshake, which he turned into a French style hug.

Daphne returned with another cup of coffee, which she placed on the table and drew up another chair.

"Please join us Sir Anthony."

"That's pretty cool Daphne. How did you know?"

"Not as cool as you finding us in the South of France when we've just arrived. But Tony looks so much like you, and I knew his father was a politician based in France."

"Yes, it wasn't too difficult, once the French Press started chronicling your exploits, after you left Paris to a fanfare. You probably never saw the papers you left behind you, on your leisurely progress but you set a few French communities by the ears.

"No harm done, and I thought it was high time my son and I had a chat in what is a neutral territory."

Daphne got up from the table and began clearing it.

"Give me two minutes, and we'll let you get on with your talk."

"I'm not sure that will be necessary." replied Sir Anthony. "If you're as close to my son as I think you are, you probably know as much of the details as I've allowed to be known" he paused, "until now. He might need a bit of comfort, and it'll save him having to explain it all to you two.

"Briefly, it is that Tony's mother isn't his real mother, although she has done a wonderful job of raising him."

There were gasps of astonishment from all three, with Tony stuttering as he tried to find words.

"I can guess what you're trying to ask, but let me explain simply."

He turned to speak directly to Tony.

"Your real mother and I loved each other from our schooldays. We were always together and both our parents understood and approved. As soon as we were 17 and old enough, we were married. Angela became pregnant almost immediately. Both families were overjoyed, except that somehow she developed a cancer which prevented her having a normal birth."

He choked a bit and reached a hand out for the glass of water Daphne offered him.

"Worse, as you Tony, became bigger we were told that unless you were aborted, your mother would die. In other words, she was given the choice, your life or hers'. She chose you."

The Double Dees were already weeping buckets, and through his own tears Tony asked, "Why did I never know? I've never even put flowers on her grave."

"It was Angela who took command of the situation. No wonder I loved her so much. She was so brave and resourceful. She said that leaving her son, how she knew it was a boy I don't know, but she did, in the hands of a bottle-feeding nanny was a mistake. What was needed was a mother who had lost her child to become his foster mother and act as his real mother. All we had to do was find the right sort of person in that situation on the day you were born.

"My father got in touch with all the maternity hospitals and midwives, explaining the situation and asking for their co-operation. ' Find a bereaved mother'. We were lucky, we found the lady who has been as good as any mother could be to you. But your birth certificate has my name as your father, and Angela's as your mother. I never married again, never found anyone to match your real mother, though your present mother is probably the nearest, and maybe I ought to do something about that."

"Maybe you should" Tony commented. "She has certainly been a wonderful mother to me."

Already the implications of this news were rushing through his mind. So he was committing no offence when he and mother shared a bed. Somehow that seemed to rob the event of some of the excitement.

"What about Nancy? he asked.

"No relation to you. She's your foster mother's mother, your foster grandmother in fact. You've got some real family grandparents dying to meet you, who are still stunned at what they've read in the papers about their grandson. It's going to take a real bit of organisation, separating one set of grandparents from the other."

So Nancy was legal after all, just as was mother, and of course they would both have known that. No wonder neither raised a fuss. He was the only one worried about his conscience. It was, he realised, a matter for celebration, not regret.

Having dropped his bombshell, Father prepared to leave.

"I'll leave you guys to discuss this news while I move into a hotel. I'll send a car to pick you up at 9-0pm, no point making a dinner appointment too early. If you've got any more questions Tony, that's the time to ask them."

Chapter Eighteen : Perfect Ending

Inevitably, it was Daphne who opened the conversation once Father had climbed into the taxi and departed.

"So, you're not quite the bastard we all thought you were!! I could never envisage you screwing your own mother and thought there had to be another answer. I'm glad I was right."

Tony thought it was best to let this version of events go uncorrected.

"Less said about all this, the better" was his only comment.

Dolores had obviously been cogitating over Sir Anthony's parting remarks.

"What do you think he meant with that remark about correcting matters vis-a-vis your" she paused, "foster mother as she now is."

Tony paused to consider. Undoubtedly it would cause an upheaval in his own domestic arrangements, but he rather liked the idea of identifying with so many other pupils at school and being visited by real parents. Sir Anthony and Lady Cole sounded rather good.

And the advantage was that no-one would suffer.

Mother, as he still regarded her, would take her own place in society with himself as her son as usual, and with his real father by her side, Ingrid and his own son in their homes in France and St John's Wood would be in constant touch with him, just in case, and Nancy, with a million pounds at least in the bank, or banks could go wherever and with whomever she wanted.

Dinner that evening at the hotel in Beziers where Sir Anthony was staying was a sensational surprise. The Double D's and Tony were led to their places by the maitre d' and were asked to stand behind their chairs. Unknowing to them, behind them came up Sir Anthony and the new Lady Cole, Tony's mother'.

"We knew." said Daphne and Dolores together. "It had to be the perfect ending. The School's going to love it."

Both had the newlyweds wrapped in their arms, while Tony stood waiting before offering his own congratulations to his newly found father, and his one time lover.

Just as well he had the apartment in St John's Wood. He didn't think that going through his mother's bedroom to reach his own would be a practicable arrangement in the future.

It was time he gave his financial adviser a call and got her involved in property on his behalf. A two bedroom flat in a new upcoming area like Brentford would be a perfect start. Property development sounded like a sensible career for him.